THE HACKER

Client. Coder. Chaos.

American writer, artist, thinker, and traveller, Stanley Moss divides his time between California, Europe and India. He is the CEO of the Medinge Group, a Stockholm-based international think-tank on branding. A graduate of the University of California, Santa Barbara, in Literature, he wrote *The Hacker* after eleven trips to India, where he researched young technology companies and the dynamically transforming culture of the subcontinent.

FiNGERPRINT!

Published by
FiNGERPRINT!
An imprint of Prakash Books India Pvt. Ltd.

113/A, Darya Ganj,
New Delhi-110 002
Tel: (011) 2324 7062 – 65, Fax: (011) 2324 6975
Email: info@prakashbooks.com/sales@prakashbooks.com

facebook www.facebook.com/fingerprintpublishing
twitter www.twitter.com/FingerprintP
www.fingerprintpublishing.com

For manuscript submissions, e-mail: fingerprintsubmissions@gmail.com

ISBN: 978 81 7234 425 2

Printed and bound in India by Nutech Photolithographers

Praise for the Book

'Here is a snapshot of the new, young and wired India, from the perspective of a clear observer, like we've never seen before. An exciting tale of betrayal, revenge, intrigue, love and passion.'

- **Henry Diltz**, noted celebrity photographer

'An unforgettable, behind-the-scenes look at new technology companies, Indian-style. There are thrills for everyone in these pages, as young executives pursue a rogue hacker through the teeming streets of Gurgaon, the temples of outsourcing, and the shadowy passages of the Delhi underworld. Impossible to put down.'

- **Allison Burnett**, author of *Undiscovered Gyrl*

'An absolute page-turner .... Racy, action packed! ... wouldn't be surprised to see this book being adapted into a movie!'

- **Dipen Ambalia**, bestselling author of
LOSER (Life Of a Software EngineeR)

'A fascinating glimpse into the clandestine world of cybercrime, where the cauldron of genius and obsession nurtures man's oldest emotion—revenge.'

- **Dr. Ronald Evans**, Professor, The Salk Institute, CA

'*The Hacker* downloads hilarity and suspense into your brain with blazing speed. Stanley Moss's vivid characters and precise satire will entertain readers far beyond the subcontinent and the digital domain. It's office drama Jane Austen would have devoured.'

- **George Rush**, syndicated columnist

'Thank goodness they've not found a way to outsource Stanley Moss yet.'

- **Yousef Tuqan Tuqan**, CEO, Flip Media, Dubai

'Kudos to Mr Moss who writes about the Indian IT underworld, where espionage and corruption overlap, with obvious disdain and yet utter fascination. His keen eye for details of Indian culture and ritual belies the fact that he's a relatively new Indophile. This is a page-turner from start to surprising finish, highly recommended and entertaining reading.'

- **Arvind Singh Mewar**, 76th Custodian, House of Mewar

This book is dedicated to
Terrence Lappin
Simon Feinberg
Richard Phelan
Safford C Chamberlain
Kenneth Rexroth

Teachers, fathers, friends.

TWO MONTHS EARLIER

In retrospect, the problems probably began not with *what* or *how*, as is usually the case in software, but with *who*. And this particular *who* wasn't the person most people would have suspected, an aggressive project manager named Shivani Sachdeva.

In late 2007, Shivani made a pitch to a Hong Kong business magnate, TK Yee, at a trade fair in the Shangri-La Hotel in Taipei. While the evening was hardly memorable for Shivani who found TK Yee's conversation bland and his breath across the table barely tolerable, the predatory businessman hungered for more from the voluptuous young woman he had chanced upon.

So he contrived a professional opportunity for her. Her employer, a young Delhi-based software company named Talsera, was offered a medium-sized contract to debug a botched software project at Yee's new tech startup in Silicon Valley, California. TK Yee's plan was simple: lure Shivani to Hong Kong on a regular basis and 'meet' her without letting his wife, five children and mistress know.

However, he never lived to see her again. In early 2008, after signing the contract with Talsera, he got embroiled in a rivalry involving his mistress—a dragon lady type who fueled the entire incident—and was murdered by a Hong Kong gangster. But the contract remained with Talsera and Shivani expected a handsome commission on its completion.

In the following spring, Shivani led a team of five programmers—two girls and three guys—to Mountain View, California, in order to understand the late Mr Yee's project. For the largely IIT-educated team, it was one of those rare on-site visits that they had always dreamt of. After touching down in the USA on Sunday, they successfully completed their assignment by Thursday, and found themselves with a full day of freedom on Friday since they were booked on a Saturday-night flight back to Delhi.

Shivani knew the city well enough, and since she was responsible for her colleagues, she told the team she wanted to show them around Silicon Valley. While the girls readily agreed to her offer, the boys declined it. They wished to ride the BART into San Francisco for the day off, a proposition which was not disagreeable to Shivani who found the boys largely a pain in the ass.

So, she took the girls to a hippy-dippy breakfast at Hobee's in Palo Alto, then to visit a cousin of hers who was a developer at Apple's corporate office in Cupertino, then lunched at the Alpine Inn, and spent the rest of the day wandering around the Stanford campus. At night she treated them to dinner at the Mission Bells Coffee Shop, which was attached to the Tropical Palms Motel where they were staying on the El Camino Real. Once she had seen the girls safely to bed in their rooms, she called up an ex-boyfriend who worked in the local eBay office and spent the night at his apartment.

The boys never went to San Francisco. Their ringleader Vikram, a reclusive twenty-six-year-old Talsera programmer, had other plans for the three of them. While the other two guys, both twenty-two-year-old provincial freshers, had spent most of their Thursday evening playing Nintendo games on the flat screen television in the room they shared and watching pay-per-view porn movies, a detail later reported by bookkeeping to the HR office in Delhi—three features, $17.99 each, listed as "in-room adult entertainment"—and which gave rise to much juicy gossip in Talsera's Gurgaon office, Vikram had spent the night in his own room, glued to his computer screen.

At Talsera, Vikram had gained a reputation as someone without a healthy balance between his personal and professional lives. Though his work was excellent, if not sometimes inspired, his behaviour was bizarre in general and truly alarming when drunk. He did not mix well with his colleagues and spent all his time hunched over his workstation at the office. On one memorable occasion, he got sloshed on Indian whisky at a Talsera company party, and challenged his imagined rivals to a finish-to-death game of *World of Warcraft*, in which he insisted he could kick their asses. When nobody rose to the dare, he came on strong to several girls at the party who immediately rejected his advances. He then stripped off his shirt, climbed atop a table and danced to "Dus Bahane Kar Ke Le Gaye Dil," before careening onto the floor and passing out.

A group of well-meaning colleagues carried him home in a taxi and put him into bed. While he snored away, they checked out the marvel of disarray that his apartment was. He was slovenly: his bathroom was a shithole; his dirty underwear was strewn all about the tiny flat; and his walls were covered with posters of Bollywood item girls, expensive sports cars, Angelina Jolie as Lara Croft and graphic centre spreads torn from *Hustler* and *Penthouse*. These details and his shirtless dance fed the gossip mill at Talsera for weeks to follow, and earned him the secret nickname "Shaitan Vikram."

People eventually got on with their work and ignored the alter ego he had revealed at the party. But HR attached him to a personal mentor. However, very soon, even he requested assignment elsewhere. When this happened, Vikram was warned he might be asked to resign if he did not learn to get along better with the people in his group at least. But Vikram's behaviour remained alienated, angry, defensive and unchanged. At the time of the California trip, Shivani was on the verge of recommending his removal from the company altogether. Though he was a brilliant programmer and a computer whiz, his sociopathic tendencies and their ill-effects on his colleagues could not be overlooked. Plenty of people wanted to work at Talsera, and he could easily be replaced.

Shivani had given permission to the boys to go sightseeing in San Francisco, but she had not known that Vikram had convinced the other two impressionable freshers to cooperate in a master-scheme of his own, one which involved neither sightseeing nor San Francisco. He had persuaded the boys to pool their money for a day of adventure, food, drinks and glamour. He had promised them an odyssey into the American heartland and an opportunity to make a small fortune in one day's time. He called it a once-in-a-lifetime chance which they would be foolish to pass up and which they would never forget. He told them he had done the necessary research on Google, and if things went according to his calculations, they would be back in Mountain View by the end of the day without Shivani ever discovering a thing.

When Shivani peered out through the curtains of her room at the Tropical Palms Motel at 6:30 a.m. Friday morning, she saw Vikram and his two charges pile into a green and white cab. She also distinctly overheard Vikram tell the driver to take them to the Denny's nearest to the BART station. Then she returned to her own preparations for a boring day chaperoning the girls and an interesting night thereafter.

She had never imagined that following their Early Bird Special Breakfasts ($5.99 - bottomless cups of coffee!), the trio of boys would ride another cab to the corner of El Camino Real and Castro, and board the Silver Dollar Special—a shiny, green, luxury-outfitted, air-conditioned bus which took people directly to Reno, Nevada, nonstop, under a special promotion advertised as "It's Your Lucky Day! Express." Vikram had found it online, where he had also easily purchased three $39.95 round-trip tickets. In the course of the four-hour ride which had followed, the two boys watched *Runaway Bride* and *The Sound of Music* on drop-down overhead video monitors. Vikram on the other hand, studied the notes he had printed out the previous night at the business centre in the lobby of the Tropical Palms Motel. All three were plied with endless drinks and snacks throughout the ride. None of them took the time to look out at the scenery.

A little before 1 p.m., the bus deposited them on Henderson Boulevard in Reno, directly in front of Earl Swaggert's Golden Ingot Casino and Hotel. Vikram turned in their coupons (*First $10 on us!*) and was handed tall plastic cups filled with big silver coins. He dispensed an additional $25 in quarters to both the boys. Then, he bought five $5 chips at the cashier's window, scoped out the blackjack tables and chose a bored-looking white lady dealer with bright red fingernails whose name tag read "Dixie" and whose ample boobs he enjoyed looking at as he played.

Fueled by complimentary Coca-Colas delivered by waitresses in skimpy outfits, the other two boys began the thrilling business of losing their 140[*] quarters, one by one, among the glittering rows of slots. It took them some time, since they were constantly distracted by the noise and lights as other people won jackpots- ka-ching ka-ching- at nearby machines. Occasionally they were visited by seductive, unaccompanied women in provocative attire, who hovered close by while they compulsively fed the shimmering slot machines. Sometimes, when the women would speak to them over the constant cacophony of the casino, the boys would blush and fumble incomprehensible replies. It did not occur to them to look for Vikram, not for hours. Only when they had finally exhausted their hoard of coins, and had repeatedly visited the all-you-can-eat buffet (*$3.99! Try our new Salad Bar!*), did they wander about the garish and windowless room in search of him. After forty-five minutes of navigating that temple of greed, where the stale smell of dead cigarettes and a thousand spilled cocktails permeated the atmosphere like a thick and nauseating fog, they discovered him deep in concentration, now at a twenty-dollar table, his chips transformed into a heap in front of him, which they, at the time, did not know totalled $6850 in winnings. For a long time they stood at the sidelines, gawking, transfixed as Vikram, seated amongst all those foreigners, bet and won, bet and won again. He did not acknowledge their presence, so focused on the cards was he.

Months earlier, Vikram had discovered online gambling from the privacy of his home in a rotting suburb of Delhi. It was an inexhaustible universe uniquely suited to his individual gifts. He was addicted in no time and even tried, albeit unsuccessfully, on several occasions to log on to gambling sites from his computer at Talsera, a detail later unearthed by IT, who routinely blocked such sites. Vikram quickly grasped the rudiments of Blackjack, and as he delved deeper into its simple principles, he realised he could easily count cards, a talent disdained by casinos but one which favoured players unknown to the house. He soon memorised the rules and the odds, and planned to try and write a program which could break the banks of the virtual casinos. But he did not know how to deal with what the virtual casinos called "token penetration." This meant he needed an enormous bankroll and had to be prepared to take a long string of losses at a brick and mortar casino before he could generate some big winnings. But, alas, he lived nowhere near a real one where his extraordinary gifts could be tested.

So, when the opportunity to do so surfaced unexpectedly in the US at the end of the Talsera trip, he quickly contrived a scheme to visit Reno. He had seen *Rain Man* and *Casino* and *21,* and he knew very well that if the casino was too small or if he demonstrated his ability too obviously, he would be quickly found out, and that, therefore, he had only one shot before being banned from any place.

When he was seated at the table in Reno, he calculated how much he could make in the time he had. The answer, when it finally came, shocked him so much that he lost sight of everything and became wholly consumed by the game.

From inside the dimly lit security room on the second floor of the casino, Sam Eldridge, the Golden Ingot pit boss, watched Vikram intently on a surveillance screen.

"That sumbitch is counting cards," he said to nobody in particular.

"How do you know, Sam?" asked a uniformed officer named Butch, whose job it was to watch the roulette tables.

"I just got a feeling. Little guy's been at it a while now—he knows exactly what he's doing. Lookee there, he just dumped a nine and a ten so he ain't winning so fast."

"You want to shut him down?"

"Nah, I can't prove anything yet. He's not wired; he's not wearing shades; he hasn't got an earpiece; and there's nothing going on between him and the dealer. His two buddies, off to the side, ain't telling him nothing neither. No, what we got here is a talented amateur. I'll shut him down when he gets to fifty. We got his picture; we'll make sure he won't be coming back."

Constantly running up his winnings and being watched by

Sam, Vikram never lost focus until someone came up beside him and whispered in his ear, "Sir, the bus has left."

"Left?" Vikram looked up as if awakened from a dream, and noted the vast, gaudy room with its red velvet walls and mirrors and its incessant din. He saw that he shared the table with a fat Chinese man; a cowboy in a white ten-gallon hat; a nervous, balding, shabbily dressed guy sporting gold chains and an embarrassing combover; and a woman wearing a T-shirt which read "I'm With Stupid So Shut The Fuck Up." He noticed the two boys he had come with, standing awkwardly to his right, and two Vietnamese call girls lurking on his left. One of them began massaging his left shoulder. The other smiled sweetly and said, "We sisters. My name Ming. Her name Ling. You and your friends want have drink with us? We go someplace, have some fun. You like have fun?" Of course it was all a lie: They were hardly sisters, simply two expats from Vietnam who worked at the casino together. They were room-mates with unpronounceable names, who sent back money to their families every month. All they wanted in life was to save up enough to buy houses in Ho Chi Minh City and return home.

"Not interested," Vikram said, removing Ming's hand from his shoulder.

"I hope your dick fall off," Ming hissed and headed for the next table. Ling followed behind.

Reality quickly came back to Vikram. He noticed that everyone—the dealer, the people around the table, the boys and a strange man in a tuxedo who stood close by—was waiting for him and at the same time, he realised that they must somehow get back to Mountain View before Shivani suspected some mischief had occurred.

"Okay, time to cash out," he told the boys. "Help me with these chips." They now represented a considerable heap. Vikram had calculated they totalled $38,980. He didn't realise that Ming had palmed a $50 chip during the shoulder massage. They walked to the cashier's window. The tuxedoed man accompanied them and never left their side. It was Sam Eldridge.

"Whyn't we let the cashier get a total for you, and you guys step into my office, please," he said, pointing to a room next to the main gates.

Vikram froze. "Something is wrong, sir?" he asked.

"When a feller wins a pot like you got yourself, we aim to watch out for him. Make certain nothing bad happens. Ain't good for business if the customers get into trouble."

They allowed themselves to be ushered into Sam's private office, a shrine to the cowboy. They were motioned to sit in three overstuffed club chairs whose leather was decorated with a multitude of cattle brands. The walls, a tribute to the Old West, were decked with rodeo posters, mounted spurs, bullwhips and frontier revolvers. A guard stood placidly, arms crossed, by the door. But Vikram's attention was focused on the tuxedoed man, a rather beefy fellow with a blond pompadour and a suspicious smile, who now sat behind the desk and played with a Bowie knife, sliding its shimmering blade between his well-manicured fingers.

"Trouble, sir? We are only customers, not troublemakers."

"Vikram sir, aapne to kaha tha koi risk nahin hai. Hum yahaan

16

arrest ho gaye to panga ho jayega, sab barbaad ho jaayega! (Vikram sir, you had said there is no risk. If we get arrested here, there would be big trouble, everything would be finished!)" one of the Talsera boys said in panic.

"*Chupbey, saaley! Mujhe baat karne de. Yeh aadmi kuchh nahi kar sakta.* (Shut up, idiot! Let me do the talking. This man can't do anything.)"

"*Mummy ko kya explain karoonga* (How will I explain this to Mummy)!" the boy whined.

Sam Eldridge didn't get a word of the gobbledygook they were saying, but he didn't care. He wanted these guys out of his casino, pronto. "No need to get all hot and bothered, son," he said affably. "We just got to sort out a few details. You'll get your money, don't worry. The cashier will draw you a cheque right quick."

"No, sir, not cheque. Must be cash."

Sam Eldridge raised an eyebrow. "Then we got ourselves a little paperwork to do first. I'll need your Social Security Number and home address."

"Sir, I respectfully request you to immediately pay me my winnings in cash. I am an Indian citizen here on a B1 visa. You can see my passport if you want."

"Whoa there, buckaroo," Sam Eldridge said, looking at the maroon ID Vikram passed across the desk. "We do things differently in the You Ess of A. See, I gotta report this to the tax man or I'm in a passel of trouble. If you ain't got a Social Security Number, then we take the taxes out right now, and neither of us hears from the IRS again."

"What is IRS, sir?"

"Now you catch that, Jimmy," Sam Eldridge said to the guard. "This feller's got some real respect going on, hear how he calls me 'sir' all the time? I like that. You one smart boy, I think. Son, the IRS is our tax office. We got a total for this gentleman, Jimmy? Paperwork ready?"

"Yeah," Jimmy said, pulling a scrap out of his pocket and consulting it. He handed over some forms to Eldridge. "After taxes he gets $27,890."

"Well now, almost twenty-eight grand! That's a pretty handsome amount for one little brown guy for an afternoon's work, wouldn't you say?"

"I surely would," Jimmy smiled.

"Sir, I am respectfully requesting that you . . ."

Sam Eldridge held up his hand. "You'll get your cash, son," he promised. "But maybe you'll give us a chance to win a little of it back?"

"No, thank you, sir."

"We'd be real happy to put you gents up at the hotel here for the night. Maybe start with a nice steak dinner and . . ."

"We are veg," one of the boys volunteered, though Sam did not understand what he meant.

". . . give you a comfy suite. Maybe you'd like to try the roulette tables? Maybe you looking for some company?"

Vikram thought: USA is so efficient about taxes! In India they would have me filling out papers for hours and then they would find something wrong and there would be days of yet more paperwork. Here they have the forms already ready! "No, sir. We will pay our taxes, and then we will go."

Sam Eldridge kept smiling. "You sure I can't interest you in a night at the Golden Ingot, on the house?"

Vikram shook his head. I know the odds, he thought. Especially roulette. Fast way to lose everything.

"I think you must be one smart guy," the pit boss went on, narrowing his cold and calculating eyes. "Maybe too smart for the people you're working for. You ever think of changing careers, taking a job at a casino? Suspect I could use a guy with your . . . um . . . expert skills." Vikram looked at the white man behind the big desk. Someday I will come back here, he thought, and I will buy this place and *you* will work for me.

Eldridge seemed to read Vikram's thoughts and sense his contempt. He passed him three sheets of paper and said, "Sign here, here and here."

Vikram perused the forms carefully. They looked official enough. One form declared the winnings, the second declared that the tax was being collected on the spot by the government and the third was a cash receipt. Vikram signed all three. The two boys gasped as Eldridge pulled out bundles of currency, counted out the balance and handed across the full amount, whistling in admiration.

"Twenty-seven eight nine-oh. That didn't hurt too much, did it?" the pit boss said as Vikram stuffed the money into his ratty shoulder bag. "Now, I been watching you play, and I don't know how you did it, but it weren't natural. I saw you give away some hands no sane person woulda let go, so I knew you was playing us along, son. I don't want you leaving us without you knowing we was on to you. Do yourself a favour: don't show your face again at

19

the Golden Ingot. Get on home to wherever it is you come from, and good riddance to you. I'm a-gonna circulate your picture around town too; let people know who you are. When you come on back here, you may find you're not so welcome. You understand my meaning?"

Vikram stared at the man and did not reply.

"And in the interest of making certain that you promptly leave town, may I offer you a courtesy ride directly to the airport in one of the casino's limousines? Is that a yes? Jimmy, call for the car. And let me offer you one more piece of free advice. The USA don't like foreign people leaving our shores with more than $10,000 in greenbacks, so if you're intending to take that money home with you, you better be certain you ain't breaking any laws, 'cause if you do you might find yourself in some unpleasant detention facility, waiting around a year and a day for some redneck judge to hear your plea. IRS is pretty interested in where gambling winnings go, 'specially when foreign nationals is concerned. So you boys better be careful. Now get the hell outta my office, your car is waiting. I got more important things to do than chew the fat any longer with the likes of you."

Shaitan Vikram was back, the two boys could see it in his face as they rode through Reno that night on the way to the airport. In the limousine, his dark side took over him and he brooded alone in the corner of the soft leather seat and fixed himself a drink of Jack Daniel's over ice from the wet bar. His other arm firmly cradled his shoulder bag, where nearly $28,000 in US currency resided.

The boys sat across from him on the jump seats. His eyes darted back and forth between them, daring them to speak, but they did not. They were wondering how they'd get back to Mountain View that night, what they'd tell Shivani and whether Shaitan Vikram, as promised, would give them their 1% of the score or not, a deal which suddenly seemed like a very unfair bargain for the incredible risks they had unwittingly taken under his urging. True, he had gotten them out of the casino, he had faced down the white man in the tuxedo and, now, due to him, they were riding in a limousine for the first time in their lives. But it had all been so reckless, deceptive and dangerous. He was correct: it was a day they were never going to forget as long as they lived, and it wasn't over yet.

As the evening descended over Reno and the limousine glided through its streets as if on a cloud of air, Shaitan Vikram sipped his drink and peered out at the glossy city of endless neon signs. He marveled at the parade of shiny SUVs whooshing by on the pristine streets which gave way to a smooth, tungsten-lit highway. All this while, as the air conditioning hissed in the background, he plotted and the provincial boys squirmed in their seats, waiting for him to issue orders.

He had told them to keep quiet until they were alone. But even in the limousine, they were not alone. The driver, a uniformed black American in a grey cap who had not said a word since he had held the door open for them at the casino, occasionally locked eyes with Shaitan Vikram in the rearview mirror. So they drove on in an eerie silence, the massive vehicle moving from lane to lane—never a bump, never a horn sounding—in the crisp and clear night air under a ceiling of shimmering stars. To the two boys, it seemed like a ride through a wicked paradise, a flight from a confused place where dreams became nightmares and where fact and fiction could not be separated.

At the airport they waited in the car until the driver got out, opened the door for them, said, "Have a nice flight, gentlemen," and drove away in silence. The boys followed Vikram to the Southwest Airlines counter, where he used cash to purchase three tickets on the next flight to San Jose Airport. The boys wordlessly marvelled at the ease with which he completed the transaction, then bought them overpriced ice-creams, found the way to the boarding gate and hustled them aboard. When the plane touched down after only forty-five minutes in the air, he led them to the outside curb, found a taxi and directed the driver to the Tropical Palms Motel in Mountain View. It was 9:48 p.m. when the cab pulled into the parking lot. All this while, Vikram had barely said anything to them.

The motel seemed to be deserted. Shivani was long gone for her assignation with the eBay programmer. The two other girls were drinking milkshakes up in their room and watching reruns of *Charlie's Angels* on television.

Vikram could see that the two boys were in a state of shock. He told them to meet him in his room on the second level in twenty minutes. Once inside his room, he pulled the currency out of his bag and counted it: $27,018 remained. When the boys arrived, he sat them down on chairs across from the queen-sized bed where the money rested, divided into three neat piles.

"Sir, it was riskier than you had said it would be. We think that we deserve a share of 10% of the winnings."

Vikram had expected this. "Two percent," he said. "Not

a penny more. It was I who signed the papers, I who will be responsible if there is any trouble. Anyway, I did not call you here to bargain. I need your help to carry all the money back to India."

"But that is an additional risk, sir. We cannot take such chances for that small a reward."

"Here is the way it is going to happen," Vikram told them coldly. "Each of you carries $9000 for me so that you don't need to declare the money to US Customs. Once we get to New Delhi, you keep $800 and give me back the rest. That is almost 3%, triple of what you expected. That is my best offer."

"Sir, let us keep $1500 each, and we are finished with you. We deserve at least that much for our loyalty and silence." The boy came from a family of rug merchants; he had seen negotiations being conducted all his life. His voice trembled as he spoke the words.

"You return $8000 to me in Delhi; that is the deal. You get the equivalent of ₹50,000. When was the last time you made that much in a day for doing nothing except having a real adventure? Take it or leave it. If you say no, I will take my chances myself, and you can each walk out of this room with $300 in cash right now, which is still more than what I had originally offered you."

The boys looked at each other and then at the money which rested on the bed in three orderly stacks. "We will give back $8000 in Delhi," they said together, picked up a stack each and left the room.

By the time they reached India, Shivani was convinced that something had happened with the boys in San Francisco. Ever since their return, Vikram had behaved in a detached way and the two other boys had sullen and secretive expressions on their faces throughout the flight back. They had avoided eye contact with her and with each other as well. Something had definitely gone wrong, she had decided. She herself had returned early in the morning, after the date with her ex-boyfriend. It had been a bit disappointing: he'd only wanted to complain about all the American girls he was dating and how materialistic they were, and how much he missed India and his mother's cooking. By the end, she decided to never see him again. Before going up to her room, she had asked the night clerk what time the three boys had returned. Ten o'clock, she had been told. She didn't think the boys could have done any serious hell-raising if they were back so early. She was sure that three underpaid boys, who had never been to the USA before, couldn't have gotten into that much trouble.

But, later, she came to the conclusion that something really suspicious had happened in San Francisco and it had all been due to Shaitan Vikram. She had decided to discuss it with Ricky Talsera once they were in Delhi. Vikram *was* brilliant alright, but clearly, he was also volatile, unpredictable and apparently led a sinister double life. He must go.

Perfect, thought Shaitan Vikram. So this is what it has come down to. He was seated in the Einstein Conference Room on the second floor of Building 3 of Talsera's Gurgaon headquarters. Waiting across from him were Priyanka, a bubbly girl from HR on the left; Ricky Talsera, the co-owner, fidgety and uncertain in the centre; and Shivani the Destroyer, seated cold as ice on

24

his right. Perfect. On the table were glasses of water, some nice biscuits and chips and the usual red folders.

They've definitely dug up something on me, he thought. Well, surprise-surprise, I will soon have a surprise for them. Vikram guzzled his glass of water, stuffed a biscuit in his mouth and sat back in his chair as if he was relaxing in his living room, watching television.

"So you understand we don't terminate at Talsera, right?" Priyanka said, leaning forward, attempting to look concerned. "We always try to create situations in which the employees can grow without stress. If somebody isn't happy, we try counselling sessions . . ."

"I know that," Vikram said, not bothering to conceal his irritation. "That was a big help. Lots of good advice, zero results."

"We put you with a mentor," Priyanka went on.

"Didn't last long," Vikram said.

"So it suggests to us—"

"Suggests to us," Ricky Talsera broke in, "that we need to get you a safety net of two or three months, use our resources and find you some new job options."

"You're firing me," Vikram responded. "Go ahead, say it. You guys want me out."

Priyanka spoke up. "We have a defined mode of disengaging a person at Talsera, Vikram. We don't give a termination letter. We treat things like this as a resignation case."

Shaitan Vikram's eyes looked up and around the room as if following a stray mosquito. He jiggled his foot, tapped his pencil on the table, and finally said, "Are you guys trying to tell me my work's not good enough?"

"No, Vikram, it's not a case of non-performance," Ricky said, obviously uncomfortable wielding the axe. "Maybe it's a difference of styles, I don't know. But whatever it is, we're trying to help you here."

"Help me?" Vikram said. "That's a laugh. You're trying to fire me without saying I'm fired. Go on, say it: Vikram, you're fired."

Shivani had heard enough. "Listen, Vikram, we've given you more chances than anyone has ever been given in this company, but lately things have gotten out of hand. Do I need to go into the details?" she asked, tapping the top of the red file in front of her with her red-lacquered fingernail. Chanel Vixen Red.

"Why don't you give it your best shot, Shivani," he said. "You've been looking for a reason to fire me for some time. What do you have on me? Stealing? Inflated expenses? Sexual harassment?"

"Some of this stuff is serious, Vikram," Ricky Talsera said. "Are you sure you don't want to just resign? Might make it easier on everyone."

"Maybe I will and maybe I won't," Vikram said belligerently. "You guys called me in here, so what's this all about?"

Shivani opened her red folder and looked distastefully at the topmost sheet. "IT was running a routine internet access audit about two weeks ago. They think you've been downloading some pretty large data over Talsera's intranet. That ring a bell?"

Vikram didn't move, just stared back at her.

"Not that it matters," she went on, "but there's been a number of pirated movies, Eastern European porn and video games coming through your address. I suppose you're going to tell me somebody's stolen your password and you don't know anything about this?"

"I'm not saying anything," Vikram growled.

"And online gambling? Sounds familiar?" Shivani asked, turning to the second page and appearing to enjoy the interrogation a shade too much.

"You guys know all this stuff can be faked. Maybe somebody's trying to get me, ever think of that?"

"Wait, let me complete," Shivani went on. "What happened on the day you went up to San Francisco with those two freshers? Some pretty wild rumours are circulating; people saying you took them to a gambling parlour. True?"

"I didn't take anybody gambling in San Francisco. Who's dreaming up all this bullshit?"

Shivani turned to the next page. "HR heard that one of those boys took two of his friends to dinner at Bukhara and left an extravagant tip behind. The other one gave a money changer, a wad of American $100 bills to convert into rupees."

Vikram stood up abruptly. "Listen, if you want me to resign, I'll resign. But not because of your ridiculous accusations." Vikram thought about the packet taped to the underside of his desk drawer at home. An envelope containing $25,000 in cash. American hundreds. He didn't need Talsera. He didn't need anybody. He could go out on his own, start his own company and compete with Talsera. He had some Talsera passwords he was already using, and with them he could easily sabotage any of their projects. Maybe even grab one of their projects out from under them. He had the power to leave little time bombs here and there, no problemo. He sat up straighter in his chair, shrugged his bony shoulders.

"You think we'd level charges like these without proof, Vikram?" Shivani snarled.

"Fuck it. I am resigning. I am so out of this place!"

Shivani watched him standing there. He's crazy, she thought. He's totally lost it. The sooner he's out of the building the better. "Okay, Vikram," she said. "Turn in your ID badge and sign the papers. Priyanka?"

Priyanka passed the papers across the table: a non-solicitation agreement and a standard letter of resignation.

"After you have signed, Hari Bhaiyya will help you clear out your desk and see you to the door. We'll send you home in a taxi, one last time."

Shaitan Vikram wasn't listening. He was bent over the table, signing the papers as fast as he could. He had a plan. He had the passwords. He could read anything he liked, post anything he liked, and now, all he wanted was revenge . . .

1

Dusk had fallen and a glowing brownish pallor settled over every surface in the city of Gurgaon, as the umber sun moved lower in the western sky, diffusing the atmosphere with a smoky veil of vapor and pollution. It was like this most afternoons in the apocalyptic city. The previous day's pre-monsoon dust storm had ripped to shreds what were once vast commercial pitches, plastered on hoardings twenty-stories high. The landscape looked surreal, like out of *Blade Runner* or *Mad Max*, the eerie evidence of a futuristic civilisation flapping in the wind, Armageddon and Utopia coexisting in one place. Gurgaon—a mad, mud city of cranes and dreams and high-rises and stainless-steel malls; a land of grandiose architectural statements; an instant metropolis populated by young people suddenly rich and getting ever richer.

Rajiv 'Ricky' Talsera turned back to the email, a memo sent by his faithful assistant Miss Briganza, on his computer screen. It read:

Coke and burgers at 6.30 today, basement lounge.
Also a charity booth there for Varanasi widows. Buy something.

SRK's new movie Pyaar, Ishq, Love at Ambience PVR at 7.30
p.m. Dinner at the mall (You can duck out on the movie, but I
recommend you go for the food.)
The following people may want to talk to you:
Pushpa, about her cab pickup point (again)
Nitin L, about ongoing problem with Shivani
Jaitendra, about another of those nasty blogposts (!)
Mr DeVries from RoodInfo LLP will be here all day tomorrow.
Senior management status review set for 2.30 p.m.

He sometimes thought she was too efficient. She kept his appointment book up to the minute, knew where to find him at any waking moment and always seemed to have her finger on the pulse of the company. Ricky glanced at the fat red folder she had neatly placed on the corner of his desk. Urgent homework again: reviewing the RoodInfo contract, more documents on the land purchase for the new campus and a frivolous lawsuit.

Another weeknight shot to hell. And Shaalu would complain if he read in bed with the lights on. She had the kids to get off to school in the morning, the house to manage, and his parents to look after, all of that, in many ways, more challenging than running a software company of six hundred people.

He wondered if Rajan Abraham had the same problem. Rajan, Khaneja and he, had together started Talsera fifteen years ago, yet Rajan seemed to have more balance in his life. Maybe it was because he got to stay locked up with the technical teams all day, and his wife Nalini didn't venture a lot of opinions. Khaneja, on the other hand, was a different story altogether: he was always on the go, troubleshooting for the company, travelling the world, drumming up new business, putting out fires and dealing with difficult clients; he was their International Man of Mystery.

DeVries was coming in from Rotterdam for the RoodInfo status review. The visit was set for the next day. An unusually tough customer, DeVries; one he hadn't yet met in person. But he had enough indirect experience with the Dutchman to dread the next day's meeting. The man was apparently volatile and opinionated and berated his own people in a cruel way during teleconferences. Moreover, he always had a complaint about the Talsera team, and protested over any fees they wanted to add, even if it was for genuine changes. But he was at the same time a big customer—Ricky had about forty people working on RoodInfo projects. The first part of the contract was worth €300,000, with possibly another million coming in over the next year. The review team had been working late nights, rehearsing for the meeting with DeVries, but there were still many things left to be fixed. As always, it was going to be a last-minute push.

Danny Khaneja was going to IGI to meet DeVries and get him settled in his hotel. Khaneja was best-suited for matters like these, as he had lived in the West for many years and had interacted with countless foreigners.

Besides, Khaneja had met DeVries in Holland on several trips. Ricky was counting on Khaneja's legendary ability to keep calm under fire, to smooth the situation with DeVries and keep him cool and happy so that the project kept moving ahead. He was hoping that a good night's sleep in a luxury hotel would put DeVries into an agreeable mood.

Khaneja had the authority to feed the guy whatever he wanted, buy him as many drinks as he desired and do whatever it took to stave off his ill-humour. It was going to be his first trip to India, his first face-to-face with the Gurgaon team. And in order to ensure that he didn't see many beggars and shanty towns on his way, Ricky and Khaneja had gone over the entire route DeVries's driver was going to take from the airport. They had rigorously studied which roads had fewer cows and where traffic would at least appear to *flow*. Besides this, orders had been issued to spruce up the entry to Building 3. Early morning the next day, before DeVries's arrival, a truck was to dump a load of loose earth on the street outside the entrance, and a team of *chhotus* had been directed to quickly fill in all the potholes. A row of hedges had been planted some months ago to hide the sewage canal next to the office, and Hari Bhaiyya had appointed local construction workers to chase off the pack of feral hogs that picked through the trash every morning on Talsera's street. With luck, the client would be spirited into the building before he was able to see any of that. Ricky had hand-picked Talsera's brightest stars to sit in on the meeting and placate the temperamental Dutchman.

Ricky looked at the next item on the memo. Nitin, one of the tech leads on the RoodInfo project, and Shivani weren't getting along well. Ricky had known this for weeks now and had been half-hoping the situation would resolve itself without his intervention. It wasn't the first time Shivani was clashing with someone junior in the company. She did some super work, it was true, yet he'd always heard from more than one source that she drove her team too hard but never gave it the credit it deserved and took all the glory herself. This had earned her the sobriquet "The Destroyer" in the company. Ricky was almost sure that Shivani was the cause of her own difficulties with Nitin, but he chose not to challenge her on it. She was an early hire and one of the few people IT had granted unfettered access to all regions of the Internet. She had also been given the latest version of every device—BlackBerry, iPod, laptop, notebook—to play with, her rewards for delivering the goods. Ricky had decided that if things got worse, he would pull Nitin out of that team and ask him to head a project of his own. He was a brilliant techie and, hopefully, mature enough to be entrusted with a complete project.

The next item on the memo: Pushpa and her cab pickup point. Pushpa, a senior programmer, had categorically refused for months to walk to the cab pickup point, a short walk from her place, though the two other girls in her commuter group had no problem in doing the same. She'd insisted that the cab pick her up and drop her right outside her home. She claimed there was a dog who terrorized her along the route. The other girls had grown resentful with this arrangement—"*Why does Pushpa get special treatment?*"

Ricky knew he'd have to deal with this situation. He decided to call HR and have somebody walk the route Pushpa objected to, get a look at the dog and see what could be done. It was one of those miniscule labour issues the man at the top should not have to deal with, but which still crossed his desk from time to time. He sent a note to Priyanka in HR and instructed her to look into it.

The final email item puzzled him: Jaitendra reporting

another anti-Talsera blogpost. That could be bad; rumours about confidential details and anti-employee policies may affect recruitment and morale. He sent Jaitendra an email asking for a face-to-face meeting the next day to learn more. A disgruntled employee at Talsera? It didn't sound right.

Ricky loaded up his backpack with the paraphernalia of the day—his battered HP laptop, fat files of papers, and the day's issue of *The Economic Times*. He headed downstairs and met some of the youngsters at Talsera on the way. He liked the way they all talked to him, and he had a lot of respect for their seriousness about their work. They were the ones who made Talsera a great place to work at, the people who kept the clients happy. They'd been very understanding about the hard times many Indian companies had experienced the previous year during those terrible months of recession. They'd all accepted temporary pay cuts, and now that the earlier salary numbers had been reinstated, they showed a renewed interest in their work. All these youngsters would be celebrating in theaters or inside pubs over the weekend, partying and cavorting, and would come back on Monday to solve the software problems of the world.

On his way out of the building, Ricky nodded at Hari Bhaiyya, who stood by the front security desk. Hari had been with Talsera since the beginning and there was a degree of non-verbal communication between them. Hari flashed a smile and returned to perusing the logbook.

His car awaited him at the gate. The driver held the door of the battered Hyundai open for him. I should probably buy a new car, Ricky thought. But then this one gets me where I need to go and is still running fine. I shall buy one when I really need one, he decided.

Stenciled on the back window of the car were the words "Drive home a relationship." That is wrong, Ricky thought, remembering his wife Shaalu. It should read: "Drive home to a loving relationship."

2

The flight attendant's shapely backside receded down the aisle of the First Class cabin. Jan DeVries sipped his champagne and wondered about her private life. He'd watched her for nine hours now as she served her passengers, her makeup perfect and her blond hair tucked neatly into place by an expert system of hair pins. Her eyes were ice-blue and her lips were the colour of spring cherries. More than once during the flight, DeVries had fantasised about what he would do with her generous bosom, buttoned tightly into her immaculately pressed blouse, if given the chance. At one point, he even debated asking her what her plans after landing in Delhi were. Perhaps if she was in Delhi for a couple days, they could have dinner together, do some sightseeing and then meet for a late drink at his hotel.

Despite his thinning hairline and crow's feet at the corners of his eyes, he thought of himself as still a moderately attractive man for 56 years old. He wore a blue shirt with white collar, a conservative Hermès tie, soft wool trousers and Gucci loafers. He had a thin Patek Philippe timepiece on his wrist, and €2000 in cash in his wallet. He had a platinum American Express card and he wore Terre d'Hermès as his fragrance. If she turned him down, it would be her own loss.

He thought back to his alcoholic wife Berthe, no doubt passed out on the couch back home in Rotterdam by now, her nightly appointment with the martini shaker over. She had gone fat and bored and middle-aged on him, and sometimes she embarrassed him in public with her slurred speech and stumbling walk. Her family's money had set them up, and she owned the house and the cars. She no longer worried about her appearance, and he had no idea how she spent her days, not that he cared about it anyway. All memories of their youth and courtship had been replaced with feelings of boredom and dread, and with late nights at the RoodInfo office and golf weekends with other executives who had similar stories to tell.

Now he was headed to India to shake up the guys at Talsera. He intended to ensure that the project was proceeding as per his directions and if it was not, he meant to threaten termination on the spot. He had heard enough of them mumbling in their strange staccato English during their conference calls, and he needed some real answers from Shivani and her team. He had another hungry Indian company in his vest pocket, pitching him for his next project. It was apparently run by some eager young man who had started at Talsera and had even been on the RoodInfo project, but was now out on his own with a new team, desperate for business and ready to play ball.

What a shame he had scheduled the meeting for afternoon the very next day. With all the crazy traffic, he was unlikely to get any time to discover the exotic delights of New Delhi or even Miss Nordic Amazon. Perhaps, if she was serving on the flight back, he would approach her for a night out in Rotterdam.

The plane touched down in the darkness. DeVries detected a faint smoky smell in the air, and it seemed to him that they were taxiing to the gate through a dense amber fog whose colour was heightened by the orange landing lights along the way. Miss Nordic handed him his elegantly tailored Italian jacket and thanked him for flying with them. DeVries thought: there would always be another flight and another flight attendant. It's a never-ending supply. God bless the ruling class; we always get everything we need.

While the ruling class was allowed to file out of the aircraft first, it soon discovered its status evaporating at the makeshift counters where masked men and women collected their H1N1 flu declaration sheets. DeVries visibly shuddered as he waited at the baggage carousel, surrounded so closely by people in odd costumes and colourful turbans that he could smell the cardamom and anise on their breath. The terminal looked like an international airport, albeit one where an unfathomable and anarchic chaos prevailed. A bitter expression appeared on DeVries's face, and he hoped Danny Khaneja was waiting outside to meet him, exactly as they had arranged.

From their first meeting itself, Khaneja had rubbed him the wrong way. The man's credentials were impeccable, and he had a fine vocabulary with only a hint of an accent when he spoke English. He was always well turned out, courteous and mannerly, and never raised his voice. During his three visits to Rotterdam,

DeVries had tried to get a better idea of the person he was dealing with, but Khaneja remained an enigma. His focus was single-mindedly on business, and he never seemed ready for small talk. Though he was comfortable enough drinking beer and eating pork sausages, he largely kept to himself. DeVries had only been able to find out that he had a young wife and son who lived in Delhi, and that his father was an engineer. As for his other interests, DeVries had drawn a blank. And as for his weaknesses, there appeared to be none. But DeVries was intent on continuing to dig.

Yet, it was with a degree of relief that he caught sight of Khaneja waiting at the barrier among the droves of chauffeurs waving their signboards announcing names of the passenger they were there to pick up. The men nodded at each other, Khaneja cracked what could be interpreted as a smile, and reached for DeVries's rolling bag, which the Dutchman allowed him to drag along.

Dilbar 'Danny' Khaneja wore grey flannel trousers, a blue blazer with brass buttons, a white open-collar shirt by Thomas Pink, a black, hand-made alligator belt that looked Italian and a pair of black tasseled Bass loafers. He was a medium-build thirty-nine-year-old and had thick hair lightly peppered with grey. Though it was now nearly midnight, he looked fresh and handsome, and projected an easygoing, confident air. Were it not for his nutmeg complexion and brown eyes, DeVries thought, Khaneja could have passed for a dashing young executive visiting the Yale Club on New York's Park Avenue. Something is fishy about this guy, he thought, and I'm going to find out what it is.

In his usual businesslike manner, Khaneja walked him across

the rough road into a dirt parking lot, warned him to watch his step at a crumbling concrete curb and at the end, held the car door open for him. When he gave the driver some instructions to take him to the hotel, Devries heard him speak in something other than English for the first time. The hotel had been a matter of contention for DeVries. He did not want to allow the Indians to put him in just any place. Ricky and Shivani actually wanted him to stay at a Radisson property near their office. But he did not trust them. "I'll take care of my own accommodation," he had told Khaneja in no uncertain terms a week before leaving Rotterdam. So, his secretary had booked a hotel that looked good enough on the Internet.

So, now they were driving through dark Delhi highways turning this way and that, beeping horns whenever they came close to another vehicle, slowing down for potholes and speed bumps, with Khaneja muttering something or the other to the driver all the while. Outside, DeVries could only gain fragmentary impressions of oddly worded signs, ghostly silhouettes of people along the roadsides, cows lingering aimlessly on centre dividers and packs of mangy dogs trotting along on the pavements. He stared at the makeshift buildings they were passing—crude constructions strewn with laundry hanging out and occasional humans huddled around oil lamps, and at hundreds of election posters in odd scripts punctuated with portraits of men in enormous moustaches, and of fat women in saris, with spots drawn on their foreheads. The driver's mobile phone suddenly broke the subdued silence of the car with a tinny ringtone, some percussive ethnic song whose words DeVries could not understand. Just then, he was sure he saw through the trees a settlement of dwellings or lean-tos covered in blue plastic tarps. Khaneja handed him a red folder of papers.

It appeared that they were heading into a zone of uneven roads and ghostly unfinished overpasses. At various construction sites, labourers seemed to be working even at this hour, carrying flat baskets of soil, with their heads covered in rags. Others stood around in groups, with nothing better to do than watch the vehicles roll by.

Perhaps it was the jet lag setting in, or maybe it was fatigue or even Khaneja's monotone, but suddenly DeVries felt tired and disoriented and irritable. He just wanted to get out of his formals, have a shower, drink a beer and crash on some bed. Whatever had possessed him to make this trip, he wondered. These were the people handling their software? And was *this* the goddamn hotel his secretary had booked? The Delhi Maharajah Palace? This place with its marble-clad façade and that kitschy fluorescent-lit lobby, and with that bored uniformed man sitting next to that metal detector? This place?

"Here's the hotel you booked," Khaneja said.

DeVries made a bitter face. "I thought it was downtown," he snarled.

Khaneja looked curiously at him. "This *is* downtown," he said.

3

It was a few minutes after noon and the basement canteen at Talsera was filled with chattering people. An hour earlier, the space—a large hall of orange walls and shiny grey marble floor, decorated with a sea of brown table tops and red chairs—had been nearly deserted. Back then, only the faint hum of the air conditioning and the occasional clatter of a pan dropping somewhere in the disorderly kitchen could be heard. Now an ambient din of conversations and laughter echoed through the room and the place was filled with a contagious energy, made all the more intense by a Bollywood music video projected onto a wall at one end of the room. Hari Bhaiyya and a canteen worker, Das, stood by an avocado-coloured barrier and watched the familiar chaos which descended there every day. To their right, in the sports room, a spirited TT game was in progress. Down past the water cooler, the Xbox room had filled up with gamers.

"You see those three girls there, Hari?" Das asked. "They always sit at that same table by the pillar, *na*?"

"Yes, they are best friends, joined the company together. That is the way it is. The best friends you make are the people you meet on your first day at work."

"That's not true with Vijay and me," Das protested. "I met him on my first day, and he and I are always fighting. I think he is a . . ." and his voice drifted off.

Hari watched the three young women meticulously take out their lunch containers from their bags, delicately open them and arrange them on the table top. He thought of them as his *teen deviyaan*, modern, educated women but still good and decent people. Even though they were a bit difficult to understand for a man from an Uttrakhand village, he knew a considerable lot about their private lives, even more than they thought he knew. It was his job to know about everyone at Talsera and anticipate what they needed, before they did.

"Yaar, you are looking at those girls again, Hari. Which one do you like the best?"

"You had better keep your thoughts to yourself. Now, go over there and clean that table," Hari said.

While Das was visiting the tables, Hari thought back to Maladevi, his wife. She lived with his parents in his native village, which was an overnight bus ride away and which he returned to only once every six months. Their two daughters were grown up and lived in different towns with their husbands.

Hari stayed at Talsera Building 3 most of the time, in a small shack up on the terrace. There he slept and cooked for himself. Even though he was paid much less than most others, he worked very hard and did more things than he had been employed to do. He supervised the work of housekeeping, kept a watch on the air conditioning, tended to the coffee machines, marked the staff attendance book, waited on Ricky and the other big folks, and made multiple rounds to the market.

Das came back. "You are still staring at those three girls."

"Never mind what I am doing."

"I would like to go to a movie with a girl like the one in the blue salwar."

To his own surprise, Hari decided to humour this outlandish thought. "First you would need to stop chewing so much paan," Hari said. "And, even then, someone like her won't talk to you. After all, you clean the tables they eat on."

"Hmm," Das said. "What do you know about her?"

Hari thought: her name is Adita, and she is engaged to someone from her own *biradiri*. She is very decent. "She is not the kind of girl you ever stand a chance with," he said.

"That's fine with me," said Das. "I was just kidding. Who is interested in her? I want someone more like the *firangi* dancer from the movie we saw last night."

Hari Bhaiyya knew more about Adita than he told Das. He knew that she had started as a trainee and was tutored by a junior software engineer named Ravi on her first project; that they had pulled the same assignments thereafter and often worked late together, side by side; that a close bond had formed between them and that now they wanted Adita to terminate her engagement and marry Ravi. She needed to come out to her family regarding this, though she hadn't done that yet. But he said nothing about all this.

"And that girl in green, I have never seen her spend a single

44

rupee in the canteen, not even to buy a coffee. Why is that? She makes much much money."

Hari thought about the girl in green, Shoba. Married, conservative, 7:30 a.m. daily pickup, always on time, always happy. But he again said nothing.

"The girl next to Adita wears jeans every day. You think she's looking for a boyfriend? Should I go over and talk to her?" Das asked.

"Of course you should."

Das knew perfectly well he could not speak to her. He envied her, because she had been to school and then to college and now she had a job, and because she could sit with her friends at a table at noon and have lunch, and wear new clothes every day and type out words on a keyboard and chat in English. She had a mobile phone on a monthly plan, and a car brought her to work each morning and took her back home each night. God has not been fair, Das thought.

He thought of the newest Honda bike he had seen under the words *Flight Into the Fast Lane*, on a skyscraper twenty-stories high. It was a sleek black and chrome beast that was also driven endlessly on television. Its advertisement showed a man riding it on an empty, straight road in the direction of snow-clad mountains, and halting it by a lake so that a foxy girl in a skin-tight leather jumpsuit could climb aboard. As they drove away, the girl shook her head so that her lustrous hair waved in the wind. He wanted that bike. He would buy one and arrive with it at Talsera one morning just as the *teen deviyaan* would be walking into Building 3. They would look at each other and ask: isn't that the boy from the canteen?

Hari Bhaiyya thought about the goddess in jeans, Harpreet. A dutiful Sikh daughter; she and a Muslim boy she had taken up with at Talsera, were about to announce their wedding. But he said nothing, again.

Hari Bhaiyya watched Das go over to their table and say nothing to any of the three as he cleared the used paper plates and beverage cans, put the empty water glasses on his tray and carried the mess out of their sight. The girls kept up their happy conversation. Over at the TT table, the boys had started a doubles game. Through the other window he could make out the Xbox jockeys jousting on their screens. The lunch tables were emptying, and the noise level was going down.

Hari thought about his own afternoon agenda: he had just been informed that the RoodInfo man had called in, something about putting things off until the next day. Now he would have to make sure that the large Einstein conference room was ready the next morning after his rounds were done. He would have to rearrange the flower pots, put the welcome banner in place, add imported coffee in the machine, ensure that the guards understood the change of plans and that everything was as it should be.

The three goddesses stood up, carefree, and left the canteen. Soon, it was deserted again, and a pleasant silence returned within its walls. Lunchtime was over. Hari went back to his rounds.

4

The Destroyer flipped open her laptop, logged in to her Hotmail account and was surprised to see a mail from Jan DeVries waiting for her.

I am in town only for a few days. I can't sleep. Would like very much to meet you for a drink. Just name the place and hour.

Shivani nodded knowingly. A drink and then he'd hit on me, just like always, she thought. Nothing ever changes, except the speed of connectivity.

Her intention had been to see Jan DeVries only at the status update meeting, and keep things formal and businesslike. But here he was, pursuing her again. The RoodInfo project was at a critical juncture. Big clients required special attention. Reluctantly she decided to meet him.

"Thank you for sending a car for me," he began, obviously embarrassed. "I admit I was not quite prepared for this place, I mean, the way things are here. I am sorry. I am a bit disoriented right now. I slept all day today."

"How did you ever choose that Maharajah hotel?"

"My assistant found it on the net."

"Fire her as soon as you get home."

It was 9 p.m. and the Radisson cocktail lounge was humming with activity. They sat at the farthest end of the bar, side by side, sipping strong drinks with witty names. "The bartender is obviously looking for a good tip," Shivani said, taking a breath. "There must an extra shot of rum in this punch. Watch out."

"You haven't written me back in some time," DeVries said. "Over the last couple of years, I emailed you a lot more than I heard from you."

"There was nothing to say, was there?"

"Maybe not for you. But I had become quite attached to you in Amsterdam. Your hasty departure really puzzled me. I always thought we were better friends than that. The way you dropped me so abruptly during our last lunch date . . . I can still see you sitting next to the window by the river, in that white dress I liked so much on you, telling me it was over, and then gone the next day. You're looking good, Shiv. And what am I supposed to think now, when you send a car for me and meet me at a bar? A drink, and then I hit on you, wasn't that always the old joke between us? Maybe tonight I'll get lucky."

"You are such a selfish pig," she said under her breath, teeth clenched. He shuddered and took another sip of his drink. She still knew how to shape the most cutting remarks, he thought. She always did, and each time he felt a peculiar thrill when he heard her say them. "You know, I am not even supposed to be *seen* with you now," Shivani went on. "You're a client. If you need help, you

48

don't email me in the middle of the night and expect me to drop everything and run to your rescue. I'm your project manager, Jan, not your mistress."

"But I had no idea the hotel would be so . . . so . . ."

Shivani looked at him fumbling there on the barstool in the multi-coloured light. He had been decent enough in Holland. It was thanks to him that she had been able to bring the RoodInfo project to Talsera in the first place. He certainly was generous and rich. Quite rich, in fact: always meeting at the nicest of places, pouring the best champagne. The only downside was that he wanted to talk far too much about his train wreck of a wife, and since she didn't really have time to humour a man twenty-five years her senior, she had said goodbye, rather abruptly, when the Amsterdam contract was over. Besides, she knew what was on his mind and she did not want to encourage him.

"You should take a room here tonight," she finally said. "Fetch your bags tomorrow morning."

"Shivani, my princess, my creator, my destroyer," he replied, putting his hand gently on her forearm, with the same over-familiarity he had employed in Holland, "if you need a place to stay tonight . . ." He ran his hand tenderly up to her elbow, and then higher on to her arm, touching her with such an intimacy that a delighted expression came over her face.

"Stop that!" she laughed, strangely flattered by his uninhibited flirtations. "Take your hand off me and order me another of those strong drinks, please."

In the darkness, Ricky Talsera stared up at the rotating ceiling fan and listened to Shaalu breathing next to him. It was at this time of the day that he could think about things and put the pieces of his life together. Shaalu constantly delighted him. She had, from the very first, been the most accommodating and affectionate partner. She acted as a calm centre of stability amidst the relentless grind of his professional responsibilities. Even after years of marriage and two children, she remained inventive in their love life. While her mature body had taken on a rounder character now, he still marvelled at how nicely she kept her skin and hair, and how her fragrances always seemed to dance seductively around her. What they had discovered in each other was mutual and private and unique. He loved her as he loved no other person on earth.

At this time, his mind, working in an exhausted body, attacked the problems of his business life from a half-dream state where the answers always came freely, quickly and clearly.

DeVries had called in sick that morning and said he wanted to rest the entire day. Initially, they were grateful for the postponement, for it gave them another twenty-four hours to fix everything they knew would probably have gone wrong, had the status review actually occurred that day. But when he also declined a dinner invitation, Ricky took note. Had he found a new supplier, someone cheaper perhaps? Had Talsera made any mistake? No, the team headed by The Destroyer was experienced and efficient and had met every deadline. He decided to wait until he met DeVries in person before reaching any conclusions.

His mind drifted back to the drinks and burgers reception of the previous night in the basement canteen at Talsera, where Nitin had blundered through the crowd and tried to start a conversation amid the hustle-bustle. "Sir, Miss Briganza said you would talk to me!" Ricky had no desire to make their conversation public. He suggested they take ten minutes in an empty conference room upstairs, and they secreted themselves away while the party continued below.

The boy was all rage when they were alone together. "Shivani doesn't know how to contain her emotions!" he said in an unabashed whine. "She takes out her frustrations on people. She is mean and vicious. Ricky Sir, I'm begging you, you got to do something about this."

"No 'sir,' please." They had dispensed with the "Sir" and "Ma'am" business. It was supposed to be all first names now. The only ones who used the honourific routinely were the new hires, but even they quickly adjusted to this detail of Talsera's corporate culture.

"You think the younger engineers don't have the experience and so they're not as good. The managers take advantage of this. They make it look as though they are the ones rescuing the project, but they are mostly clueless. For example, Shivani never gave any of us credit for the Pharmacom job that was such a success last year. It was the team that made all the difference in that one, not her." He didn't get a promotion, and he didn't get an increment, Ricky remembered. Why would he stay? Ricky had read about him in the overly detailed HR report.

Lives at home, only child. Father retired, mother housewife, his salary runs the home, no car, gives his mother money for groceries. Claims he doesn't want to get married. Says he idolises Einstein and Mother Teresa, but also Hitler! Uncertain about his career path. Mainly wants to increase his salary.

In the same report, The Destroyer had written: "…performance unsatisfactory. Will recommend his resignation at end of month, after he returns from sick leave."

In the conference room, Ricky realised he too could be convinced that the easiest path would be to get rid of Nitin. He looked rather obviously at his watch, but the kid didn't take the signal and kept blabbering. At last, he had to interrupt him. "I really have to go now, Nitin. Let's rejoin the party. I will look into the matter later."

"Yes, okay, thank you, sir. I have really benefited from this talk."

Later, he had met Jaitendra at the chai wallah's stall across the street from Building 3. It was an irregular ritual he had known for years. The stall offered them a space where they could grab a pair of plastic stools under the awning, lean in close to each other, take a cup of chai, share a packet of potato chips and confer undisturbed.

At forty-four, Jaitendra was older than most people in the company and had seen much more of the world. Years earlier, when he had joined the company for zero pay in return for the right to work on software, Talsera had just been a startup in a dingy little office. Now, years later, he had shares, seniority and tremendous respect as an architect and manager at Talsera, even though he wasn't one of the men at the top of the org chart. His loyalty to the company was legendary; he was known to match the young hires hour-for-hour on difficult projects. If you wanted to lobby Ricky Talsera indirectly, there were few better ways than to get the ear of Jaitendra.

"This second blogpost is nastier than the first one. Claims we are a sweatshop and are cutting corners on a certain project out of Holland. Attacks the woman in charge, who bears a shocking resemblance to . . ."

"The Destroyer," Ricky guessed.

"Correct. IT has figured out it came from a shadow Hotmail account. Untraceable. It's also pretty uncomplimentary about working conditions."

"What do we do next?"

"My instinct tells me that we wait. They're obviously targeting RoodInfo. Let's see if the client lets on to any knowledge of this tomorrow. I have IT watching for anything suspicious originating from our laptops or from within our firewall. We can't go public with this for now. We can only hope it goes away."

"Okay," he said to Jaitendra. "Keep me posted, and let's hope they don't pop any surprises before the status review. That could be a disaster."

After this, he headed home to the island of stability that was his remarkable wife.

5

The young man sat on the open verandah, sipping tea and staring at the marble floor. The verandah fronted a three-storey house on a tree-lined street in one of the residential districts of Gurgaon that had been hurriedly built in the last decade and was already showing the ravages of harsh weather and pollution. But the porch was shady and the afternoon mild, and from his elevated position, he watched the occasional passage of cars and bicycle rickshaws and considered his options for the future. For a handsome twenty-six-year-old man, he seemed overly troubled. His concern centered on a young woman inside the house, someone he thought about constantly now. He had grown particularly fond of her as the months had passed, and now liked her more than any other person he had ever known.

Now, as he waited for her outside Gupta Aunty's PG, where the young woman lived, his mind went back over the hours they had spent shoulder to shoulder, working late nights at the Talsera office, and how their affection had grown over tea breaks and stolen glances at company events. He smiled as he recalled how he would watch her jealously during her salsa classes, how he would feel an irrational rush of possessiveness come over him when another developer would stop by the lunch table to speak to her about inconsequential project details.

It was the first time in his life that he had looked at another person in such a way. Suddenly, he was acutely aware of everything about her—how easily amused she got by the dumb jokes her friends told, how she always added three cubes of sugar to her coffee, how her slim fingers danced over the keyboard gracefully, how she found time to stop at the temple and ask for Krishna's blessings, how softly she spoke to anyone who sought her counselling, how seriously she took her job and how everyone seemed to love her but none as much as he did. Every aspect of hers fascinated him. He found himself transfixed by the way the afternoon light fell on her hair, by the colour of the shawls she chose, by the melody of the popular songs she hummed, and by the lightness of her step as she drifted among the cubicles.

Love was a word he had never entertained before, but in Adita's case it had appeared one day, in a flash-like sudden lightning. He had taken his time in declaring it to her. He endured it for countless dark nights, lying alone in his small bed in his tiny room in the apartment he shared with his friends, wondering and wondering, before finally blurting it out to her one evening as he escorted her to the cab. She had stopped in her tracks and had admitted that the same was true for her as well, thereby opening the floodgates of complications—how were they going to continue under the circumstances?

He was not worried about his parents. He knew they would

understand, since they themselves had a love marriage, an act at first opposed by their own parents, and not typical of their generation. His father owned a small marble cutting and trading business in Ahmedabad and his mother had given up a career to raise her children. They had sometimes broached the subject of marriage with Ravi, but he had always said he wanted to wait.

Adita's family was certainly going to be infinitely more difficult. Her family came from a tiny town outside Jaipur, a very conservative place where they had been living for more than a century. Without even asking her, they had selected a groom for her. She was to return home during Diwali to meet her future in-laws. It was unthinkable for her to defy her parents. But now she had fallen in love.

Two weeks earlier, Adita had sat helplessly inside her room, in a shaky old chair. On the weathered wooden table before her, lay an unfinished letter. She needed to make her father understand that she lived in a big city where women now married the man of their choice and that there was nothing wrong with love marriages or marrying outside one's caste. They would need to understand. After all, it was they who had sent her to the school where her marks bettered all the boys', they who had encouraged her to crack IITJEE, and they who had sent her away from home to study once she had cleared the exam. If she earned and sent a decent amount home each month, did she not also have the freedom to choose her husband?

Dear Papaji, thank you for your last letter. I apologise for not writing back as quickly as I have always done. Actually, we have been finishing a large project at work and I have been really busy with it . . .

She hesitated and looked at the hollow words she had written. He would see through them. She crumpled the paper into a ball, tossed it into the dustbin and started all over again.

Papa-ji, you have always taught me to follow my heart and speak honestly . . .

Again she discarded the paper and stared down at a new blank sheet. The enormity of her decision was suddenly clear to her. She was trying to move heaven and earth at the same time. Tears appeared in her eyes and fell on the blank page, tiny pearls among the light-blue lines. For these past two years she had lived in Gupta Aunty's PG, with a few other girls who sometimes stayed out all night with their boyfriends. She, on the other hand, had remained single all this time. But her heart told her now, that it was time for her life with Ravi to begin.

Out on the porch, Ravi considered the pain he knew she was going through. She had written to her father two weeks earlier, but no reply had come as yet. He hoped that she had found the right words. He had big plans for the night: a visit to their favourite *aloo-tikki* stall, then a rickshaw to the mall where he was going to show her the ring he had chosen at a jeweller's store for her, and then a romantic movie at the theater. He felt an innocent elation at the thought of their elbows touching, of their hands finding each other in the darkness of the theater. Perhaps tonight they would discover a moment to kiss. He was sure she would cry during the blatantly sentimental scenes, as she always did. Later he would drop her at the door of her PG, and under the leafy moonlit shadows, he would kiss her again and say goodnight until the morning.

Safe in his fortress of solitude, Shaitan Vikram plotted. After leaving Talsera, he had spent countless hours in the same dark space, reading, watching, and waiting. He had left Talsera with passwords nobody knew he had taken. Now he could read anything on Talsera's net, even private interactions between the very people who had forced him to leave. He knew where the bugs in the RoodInfo project were, and had already left a few time bombs of his own in the code. And then there were his anonymous blogposts. He wanted to ruin The Destroyer, drive the client into his own virtual arms and take the project away from Ricky Talsera, all the while remaining unknown, unseen, untraceable, and undefeated. Once he had accomplished his sinister aims, they would all be left shaking their heads in wonder: "What the hell happened?" But they would never find out. Vikram would be a digital spectre; no trail left behind, his identity forever a mystery. All the profits would be his and only his. Everything would be transferred to hidden accounts, moved from bank to bank, impossible to trace. He would build a secret palace somewhere far from Gurgaon and from there he would operate his own global empire. He would fly first class, party with movie stars in his own nightclub and drink seven-year-old single malt whiskies surrounded by the hippest people.

He opened his anonymous Hotmail account and began to write a new blogpost.

Hate it here at Areslat. The managers are useless and the senior partners pitiless. They act like they care about their people, but to them, no one really matters. They demand late nights and weekend work and people actually go along with it. The top dog says he is interested in

everyone. But try and talk to him, he does nothing. They put you with
mentors who steal all the credit.

This Dutch project is a joke. It's badly written and filled with
bugs. They tell the client it's ready for release, and then they run around
bumping into each other to get it looking like it's done. Big status
review tomorrow, and everything's a mess. The remote sync is definitely
not working, for example, and how can it? It's designed wrong. Let's
see if the client finds out.

Shaitan Vikram hit the "publish" button and the message uploaded instantly. He smiled to himself, cackled sinisterly, logged out and loaded up the latest version of *World of Warcraft*. A little game for old times' sake. He called himself KnightTuring. He would blow away a few armies and later get back to the RoodInfo sabotage. In many ways, he preferred blowing up the real world to the virtual world. The Destroyer and Ricky Talsera had ruined his life, and now he had a clear mission: to destroy Talsera and thrust upon Ricky a humiliating defeat, much like the dragon he was about to slay with his exceptionally large battle axe.

"Someone has definitely been reading our internal mail," Jaitendra said, in his matter-of-fact way, as if he were discussing the weather. He was seated at the chai wallah's, in his usual red plastic chair, with a packet of tikka masala chips open on the table in front of him. He held up the packet for Ricky Talsera, but Ricky didn't take any. "IT sent a group of dummy messages and somehow figured out that the guy has been reading *everything*. The problem now is that we know the blogger knows, but we can't let on that we know, or he will know we know."

Ricky Talsera sipped his chai. It was early evening and a more leisurely rhythm prevailed on the deserted streets. A twitching dog slept on its back, next to an orderly row of two-wheelers. Overhead, tall swaying eucalyptus boughs loomed, their leaves casting flickering irregular lattices of orange and black on the street below. From down the road they could hear the percussive sound of a Punjabi song on the radio. Somewhere in the distance, two men argued about the outcome of a test match. Nobody bothered them. "We must keep our letters looking like business as usual," Ricky said. "Until we locate this creep and shut him down, we can't stop talking about RoodInfo amongst ourselves. We will have to keep our suspicions hidden and our messages vague. From now on, all our real communication will have to be done face to face."

"Correct," said Jaitendra.

From across the street, Security Guard #8 Raheem watched them through the tiny window of his wooden shack by the entrance. Very unusual, he thought, both sirs meeting two days in a row. He and his colleague, Security Guard #13 Vartan, concluded that it had been months since they had seen this happen.

Ah, the dinner table, the centrepiece of Rajan Abraham's enviable home life. His daughters—the younger one an embodiment of mischief at ten and her sister a brooding mass of teenage hormonal activity—incessantly delighted him with their theatrics, while their mother impressed him daily with her towering managerial skills and her culinary artistry. Perfect world! This was Rajan's private theatre to which he alone was audience, he alone a witness to the epic struggle between the mother and the daughters, who would all be vying for Daddy's attention. What a blissful position, Rajan thought. A man with two daughters is truly blessed. He had only just speared a tender morsel of chicken and added a touch of Nalini's famous pickle when his BlackBerry, which sat by his glass of water, began to buzz and slide towards the edge of the table. It was a message from Ricky.

He opened it immediately, force of habit after so many years of working together. "Sorry, I need to read this," he apologised. The buzzing had interrupted an urgent conversation about new outfits to be purchased for Diwali. "It's from Ricky."

Rajan got out of his chair and walked to the terrace where the reception was good.

Someone's hacking our email. I have some ideas. Can you talk now?

He hit the autodial and heard Ricky's mobile ringing. How different the old times were, he thought, when there were no cell phones. One had to wait for months and years for landlines. There were also those occasional two-hour VSNL network outages which everyone loved because they thought of them as a nice little break. Now Ricky Talsera, no matter where he was, was only a few seconds away.

"Raj, where have you been?" Ricky said when he picked up the call.

"Mostly reviewing RoodInfo and rehearsing with the team. I think we're looking good. You saw those ugly blogposts?"

"Of course I did. People can't stop talking about them. Do you have an idea who might be behind them?"

"Needs to be someone with inside knowledge. Seems like someone who has worked on the project from the start."

"It's not The Destroyer. She can't be killing her own commissions. Unless she's about to jump ship on us, but I don't believe that is the case. The blogs are pretty technical. My hunch is that it's a techie. I think I know who it is. Maybe a certain former techie."

Rajan Abraham went silent. Immediately a text appeared on Ricky's handheld screen.

Rajan: *Put Jaitendra on him, have him watched. Do the same for our foreign friend.*

Ricky: *I'll get Dilbar on it immy*

Ricky: *Can IT track the hacker?*

Rajan: *One guy says he thinks he knows how*

Ricky: *Try it*

Ricky: *Will call now*

Rajan: *Okay*

"Raj, you guys need to come over for dinner, like in the old days. Shaalu also says it's been too long."

"I know. I don't have to tell you how crazy things are at the moment. The kids are growing up. And my house is always like a railway station, everybody coming and going. And boy has our company changed! When you grow this fast, things are bound to go out of control."

"I know. You remember when we first started? You used to unlock the front office gates every morning. Thank goodness Hari Bhaiyya does it now."

"Oh, yeah, I remember how crazy we were back then. Used to work even on national holidays!"

Rajan laughed. "Man, I miss those days."

Ricky paused for a moment, reflecting. "And do you remember those insane marathon ping-pong games we used to have?"

"Oh yes! People would always line up for a turn. At least we have two tables in the canteen now."

"Rajan, do you remember Harinder? That new guy last year who said he could beat everyone? I think he worked on RoodInfo for a while."

"Yes, no one liked him at first, did they?"

"No. But it amazed people when he beat them all left-handed. Turned out he'd played at state level in school. People kind of resented that."

"But they loved to watch him play," Raj said. "So whatever happened to him?"

"Infy, I think. He's down in Bangalore now."

"Hey, wait, if he started on the RoodInfo project, maybe he's the blogger?"

"I don't think so. He ultimately made friends here, and he didn't leave with any grudges either. Besides, the project has come a long way since he left. I don't think it's Harinder."

"Maybe HR should call him and see what he's up to."

"Maybe Khaneja should. Pretend we want to hire him again. Find out if he knows anything. What's that noise?"

"Nalini and the girls, arguing about Diwali. I must get back and mediate. It's my money they're fighting over after all. Chal, yaar, talk to you later. I gotta go handle this or else it's gonna cost me a fortune."

Danny Khaneja sat in his office, his phone glued to his ear. As usual, he had a diverse list of timely items. As always, Danny needed to work on them in his own way, at his own speed.

Khaneja was the first person Ricky and Rajan had called many years ago, after founding the company. Khaneja had taken a big chunk of equity in exchange for his business savvy and contacts. He was a silent owner, and yet a driving force in the company. He liked Ricky and Rajan, and he liked letting them run things. He acted as the go-to guy, the problem solver, the big picture strategist and the occasional henchman. And he relished the freedom his low profile afforded him. People knew he influenced policy, but they did not know how he fitted into the hierarchy. He was loved by some and unknown by others, and consequently, happily misunderstood. It had always been thus, and he loved it that way. He dialled the first number on his hit list.

"Hello, you have reached the office of Dr Narayan at the Friends Colony Clinic for Reversal of Aging. I am presently unable to speak to you, so please leave me a message after the tone. If this is an emergency, you may dial star and my service will page me. If you wish to make an appointment, press the hash key."

"Doc, Danny Khaneja here. Listen, you old sawbone, a lady is in her doctor's office after an exam. Doctor says, 'I'm sorry to tell you this, but you're going to die in six months.' Lady says, 'Well I want a second opinion!' So the doctor says, 'Oh yeah, here's a second opinion: you're ugly.' Call me when you can. Same number as usual." Click.

Danny made his next call.

"Namaskar, Hotel Delhi Maharajah Palace. May I help you?"

"I'd like to arrange a taxi this afternoon for your guest Mr DeVries, please."

"Mr DeVries-ji has checked out, sir."

Danny Khaneja sat upright, stunned. Hesitated.

"Sir?"

"Mr Jan DeVries from Rotterdam?"

"I am sorry. He checked out this morning. Has changed to the Radisson Gurgaon."

"*Theek hai*, thank you," Danny said and hung up. Nice of him to let us know, he thought. I think it's time to check with The Destroyer. It's a pain to talk to her, but I'm sure she knows what is going on with DeVries

Danny dialled Hari Bhaiyya's number. "Hari, I need you to find where Shaitan Vikram lives these days and keep an eye on him."

"*Theek hai*," said Hari Bhaiyya. "You know the driver Suresh? He saw him recently. I will take his help and find Vikram for you."

Danny hung up. I'm sure you will, he thought.

In Room 481 at the Radisson Gurgaon, Jan DeVries lay peacefully soaking in his bath. Things seemed to be going well, now that he had escaped that rat-hole of a hotel. He had gotten drunk with Shivani the previous night, but she'd gone home in her own car quite late. He had made an early trip to the old hotel in the morning to retrieve his bags. On his way back, the effects of jetlag suddenly became apparent. Ahh, how positively delicious it was to return to the Radisson and immerse himself in a hot bath. Suddenly, his titanium Vertu phone buzzed. It was an SMS from 'Competition.'

I have some imp information for u, useful before your Talsera meeting later today. It is time we met in person. KnightTuring

DeVries smiled pleasantly to himself. Things were getting interesting. Let's see what the competition has to offer, he thought. Let's get a look at them up close. Shivani said the status review is going to go fine. Perhaps there is something else I need to know before I walk into that room.

Rotterdam had been forwarding him the negative blogposts about Talsera, but DeVries hadn't thought much of them. They didn't reveal sufficient information. He had plenty of experience with disgruntled employees and knew enough to discount whatever internet posts, like the ones being forwarded to him, had to say.

But, he still wanted to check out this KnightTuring company. Maybe they really had something to offer. He wondered if he would finally be able to talk Shivani into the sack after all these years.

As this idea crossed his mind, Jan DeVries heaped a load of bath bubbles onto his head in utter contentment and sank down into the deliriously warm water until he was completely submerged.

7

"Let me off here," Priyanka said to the driver. "And now remember what I am telling you. Drive some distance behind me as I walk. If you see any dog get near me, come to my help quick, quick. I think I will reach the cab pickup point in ten minutes."

With this, she stepped out of the car and peered cautiously in both directions. Nothing suspicious. It was 6:50 a.m. She was wearing her running shoes, just in case. She did not know how large a dog to expect. Pushpa had neglected to provide its description in the issue tracker. In her imagination, Priyanka visualised a terrifying creature out of *The Hound of the Baskervilles*, a huge, rabid mass of fur with blazing eyes, sharp, glistening teeth, wildly barking and rushing towards her. She set off down the road with admirable determination.

To her left she caught sight of the house where Pushpa lived, a multistoreyed bland structure that could be both forty years old or brand new. You could never tell a building's age in Delhi. Pushpa would be upstairs, probably at the breakfast table or brushing her hair at the moment. The Talsera cab would pick her up in forty-five minutes. Priyanka recalled the report from HR which she had studied the night before.

Pushpa says a wild dog threatens her on the way to the pickup point in the morning. Wants the cab to pick her up from her place. Says she is afraid to walk. I have temporarily approved a driver pickup because of her seniority.

But, the two other girls on Pushpa's route are quite upset that she gets a pickup while they don't. I have received complaints from both of them on this. I spoke to Pushpa, but she insists the dog frightens her. She says the route is very unsafe.

True, it was not the prettiest of streets. All manner of buildings stood on either side. Businesses lined the street level, most shut securely behind metal shutters, a succession of identical red telecom logos painted outside each. On the walls and pillars of the street, thousands of other advertising signs had been plastered, covering every available inch. Stretched digital banners, illustrated with garish photography, competed with hand-made signs and peeling paint for space everywhere. Dangling power and telephone wires hung randomly and dangerously like draped black spaghetti. Balconies strewn with laundry hung out to dry on metal wires, told a thousand life stories about the inhabitants of each house.

Some businesses—roadside food stalls, pharmacists, dairies, tailors and mechanics—had opened early and awaited the first customers of the day. Out at the edge of the pavement, fruit and vegetable sellers had set up their carts, stacking them high with pyramids of fresh produce. Two cows sprawled peacefully next to a long puddle, their jaws rotating in unison. Traffic was minimal; the streets were deserted except for a few cycle rickshaws, a couple of careening school cabs and an occasional scooter. Some people stood in line at a small corner shrine.

A city awakening. It was about the most non-threatening scene Priyanka could imagine. A few stalls down, a shopkeeper stood at a single gas stove, with layers of eggs stacked neatly to his left. The sound of hooves momentarily distracted her: an equestrian on a freshly-groomed and plaited white horse galloped by, frisky in the morning, perhaps being exercised before the streets became too crowded, perhaps on his way to a farmhouse across town for someone's wedding that night. She admired the professional way the rider sat on his horse, so regal and straight-backed.

"Bread omelette?" the omelette wallah offered.

Priyanka sized him up: gaunt, sparse moustache, sinewy forearms, an open-collar white khadi shirt and wrinkled khaki trousers; probably here every morning, has a lot of eggs to sell, must be popular. "Thank you," she answered. "I have already had my breakfast. I want to take some parathas with me to my office. Where can I get good ones?"

"There's a man down by the bus stop. He uses good ghee. Try his radish paratha."

"Is it always so busy this early?" she asked.

"This is busy? In one hour you won't be able to even cross the road!"

"I hope there are not many dogs around," Priyanka ventured. "I am quite frightened of them."

"No," the man protested. "No dogs here. We scare them away with sticks and they never come back."

"Hmmm, thanks," she said and walked to the paratha wallah's

stall. The omelette-seller had been correct: the parathas smelled delicious. She ordered a few to carry with her. As the paratha wallah began to shape the dough and wrap it around the filling, she looked around again, observing the route Pushpa did not want to walk.

"This is such a quiet street right now," she said to him. "But it must get quite crowded later, no?"

The man looked up from making dough balls. "Yes, not very busy in the morning generally," he said. "But by afternoon it is jam-packed. I get a huge crowd at lunch. Touch wood!"

"Are there any dangerous dogs here?"

The paratha wallah regarded her curiously. "Are you from some government office?" he asked. "The Municipal Corporation or some NGO?"

Priyanka laughed, instantly disarming the man. "No," she said innocently. "I'm just afraid of dogs." The man concentrated on the parathas, waiting for the correct moment to turn them on the *tava*. Their aroma was intoxicating. He did not look up. "No dangerous dogs here," he said simply. "You should not be so scared of things."

"Your parathas smell so good!"

"Our family recipe," he looked up and grinned.

Some school girls now marched in groups along the lane, their uniforms freshly pressed, their sashes expertly draped to fall shoulder to opposite hip, their hair done into two tight braids. I had a uniform like that once, Priyanka thought. The schoolgirls did not appear the slightest bit concerned about hostile animals.

She glanced behind and saw her car holding back at an

appropriate distance. A typical neighbourhood, she thought, nothing bad seems to be going on here. A hundred metres down, at the end of the road, next to a stretch of open fields, she could see the spot where the Talsera cab stopped. Priyanka steeled herself. This is the last stretch, she thought. If the threatening canine is waiting to attack, the stand-off would occur here.

She paid the man, stowed away the parathas in her shoulder bag, and resolutely went forward to see whether Pushpa was labouring under a hallucination or simply telling a magnificent fib so she didn't have to walk, or were there really big dogs around.

"Khaneja, Narayan here. Getting back to you finally. Sorry, I was away for the week at a conference in Singapore. You never saw so many plastic surgeons in one place, hahaha. Did you get in another fight with a Nigerian? I hope not. I thought you healed up fine last time. Listen, a guy walks into a doctor's office. The doctor says, 'I've got good news and bad news.' Guy says, 'What's the bad news?' Doctor says, 'You've only got six months to live.' Guy says, 'Oh my God, then what's the good news?' Doctor says, 'See that really cute nurse out there?' Guy says, 'Yeah . . .' Doctor says, 'I'm sleeping with her.' Hahaha! Anyway, I hope you are behaving yourself. Stay off the pain killers. Try me tonight at home, and please keep out of trouble. I don't want to have to stitch you up again."

Shivani regarded her naked self in the mirror. Perhaps she had put on a few pounds since returning to India. A small roll of fat had certainly grown around her middle. She wondered if it would prevent her from landing a captain of industry who could keep her in style for the rest of her life.

She examined her boobs carefully, pushing the skin above each in turn, then both together, wondering if a little lift was needed. It was certainly affordable enough and she even knew of a fine clinic outside Geneva where she could hide away for two weeks after the surgery.

The woman in the mirror had little in common with the naive girl who had joined Talsera after her bachelor's so many years ago. That was a girl who only wore cheap denims and embroidered salwars and kept her long hair braided down her back. She remembered all too well her initial, interminable days of bad clothes and awful washrooms and network outages and rickety old office vans.

In those days Talsera was rapidly growing, and there was more work than people to do it. You took whatever job was handed to you. Within a few months of her joining, she found herself dispatched to Holland to manage a project for a Dutch company called RoodInfo. A twenty-two-year-old girl, who had never been outside India and who had never lived alone either, was suddenly travelling in jets and modern trains and living in a sublet apartment in Amsterdam. Sometimes she would even venture to nearby countries with her RoodInfo friends. Everywhere, she encountered people drinking alcohol and smoking cigarettes. She soon joined in.

It was a dream existence, a living out of fantasies she had only seen in movies. But the dream came to an abrupt end when during a phone call, her mother revealed that her father was searching for a prospective groom for her and that they wanted her married by the end of the year. Of course she had no desire to marry so soon. But it was unthinkable for Shivani to refuse her parents. She realised she only had a few months of freedom left. When she pictured herself domesticated and married off to a suitable stranger, thousands of miles from the glamorous cities she had come to know, she decided to spend the remaining time in Europe unrestrainedly, living life to its fullest. She started staying out late, frequented wild parties, drank with abandon, and began making as many new friends as possible.

Without her knowing, an obvious aggression gradually became a part of her everyday manner. If she ultimately had to give up this professional life, she thought, then she would take no prisoners. This attitude infected her work, and she soon gained the reputation of being a vicious player who would do anything in business to win. She did not care when she learned that people at the home office were now calling her The Destroyer.

Perhaps it was her overt toughness and sudden transformation which caught the attention of Jan DeVries, the CEO of the very company she was working with in Holland. He had started out with her rather formally, but then began to invite her to lunch every week, each time a new restaurant, and always the finest ones. At first, she met his interest with professional eagerness. They sampled dining rooms in classic hotels, tried local delicacies at country inns and ordered dishes with unusual names at luxury chateaux. Eventually she began to meet him in other cities as well. He covered all her expenses, and she always had her own hotel room.

Jan DeVries was worldly and Shivani observed him closely. He knew how to talk to a sommelier, which fork to use and which wine to order. He always knew the fruits in season and, so, could order the sweetest desserts. He proved to be an encyclopedia of interesting and unexpected information for her.

"See how elegant that Italian woman looks?"

"Jan, how can you tell she is Italian?"

"Look at her shoes, her bag, the tailoring of her leather jacket and the scarf. Florentine? Milanese? Definitely not from the south." DeVries refilled her glass with bubbly.

"And what about that man over there, what do you think, Jan?"

"Oh, he is a Brit, isn't he? Looks like a shady banker moving some big money around. Well, the shoes are right, and he has a bad haircut; an old bespoke pin-stripe, but good cloth, and it's double-vented, probably Saville Row."

"Jan, you amaze me."

"Shivani, dear, it would be a travesty to let the last of this noble Cliquot go to waste. After all, it's the perfect pairing with your *tarte aux fraises du bois*."

After enough of these long, lingering lunches, it became unmistakably clear what he wanted from her in Amsterdam. She began to detect a pattern in his behaviour; it was quite predictable. He would first converse about interesting things during the meal, as he filled her full of expensive wine, and then over desserts he would ask her rather bluntly, sometimes even crudely, to come back to his room with him. She would always refuse. He was so old, and from the West, and was married. Yet, in a disarming way, she found DeVries attractive. He was a source of amazing weekend trips, remarkable meals and a wealth of reliable industry information.

By the time the project wound down and she was assigned next to go directly to Silicon Valley, California, on a new project, her initial fascination for him had turned to disdain. She told him what she thought of him without restraint. But the more searing and scathing her criticism became, the more he seemed to like it. There was no sport in taunting him. She decided he would never be able to get her into bed.

She said an abrupt goodbye to him in Amsterdam. It was over lunch at La Rive, at the Amstel Intercontinental. He had chosen a table overlooking the river. He took the news coolly, congratulated her and said he hoped they would stay in touch. Shivani said she was sure they would. He asked her if she would consider more work on the RoodInfo account. Talsera was already bidding on a new project with them and he had the power to throw it her way. She said that was fine with her, but he should not count on seeing her all that much even if that were to happen. The next day she flew off to America, her first time there. She was twenty-five years old.

When she was in California fate intervened again. Her parents were killed in a mad stampede of worshippers during the descent from the holy cenotaph at a Karnataka shrine, where they had gone for a pilgrimage. Shivani was summoned back to Delhi for the funeral, but things were so complex that she could not immediately settle their affairs. She returned to California midway and lost herself in her work, awaiting the Byzantine paperwork of the estate to be assembled.

A young Indian programmer at eBay in Mountain View appeared to take pity on her and comforted her in her hour of grieving. He was so handsome and persuasive that she fell into a torrid affair with him, losing her virginity in a blaze of passion. The next few months were like a Bollywood romance, with dramatic conversations played out on picturesque Californian backgrounds—Big Sur, the Golden Gate Bridge and Disneyland. He took her shopping to GAP, Banana Republic, Abercombie & Fitch, and Nike. They watched American TV shows together in the evening and jogged on the running trails along the San Francisco Bay in the morning. They went to late-night shows of uncensored adult movies. Shivani, now accustomed to making her own decisions, even tasted hamburgers, beef and all.

But when the project ended, Shivani needed to pack and return to India. Her hope was to be done with the business of the estate once and for all, and return to the Bay Area and to the arms of her lover as soon as she could. The programmer from eBay however, took the news differently than she expected.

"Shivani," he said, looking up from his Game Boy, "you go back and do what you have to do. It's not gonna be easy, but I know you can do it. When it's all settled, call me up and we'll hook up again," and immediately went back to disintegrating a row of aliens on the screen in fiery blasts. "And can you, please, grab a Dr Pepper for me the next time you come back from the kitchen?"

Stung by his dispassionate words, Shivani returned to India angered. But, when she reached home, avaricious lawyers and cousins descended to pillage the estate. After months of complex legal battles and struggles with foxy relatives, Shivani emerged victorious. The combat had turned her into a relentless fighter.

Her parents had lived comfortably, it turned out, and she was shocked to discover at their passing, just how many millions of rupees and dollars and euros they had collected in substantial accounts all over the world. And since she was the only child, she had inherited everything. From that point onward, she also realised she would be on her own for her entire life.

Late one night, at a hip Delhi nightclub, a Nigerian student sold her a small quantity of primo Colombian flake. She loved the effect it had on her. It became her habit, which could have gotten worse, but didn't. During these go-go days, Shivani began to frequently travel internationally to places like Taipei, New York, Los Angeles and the Côte d'Azur. She never called Jan DeVries again.

But when he emailed her out of nowhere, to meet late the previous night, she decided to give him another chance. Thanks to him, the second big RoodInfo project had come her way. Besides, her virginity was no longer an issue.

The evening had gone fine. As expected, he had tried to get into her pants, but she had rebuffed him as always. He was so intoxicated that she had to steady him as he stumbled up to his room. He had tried to kiss her messily in the elevator, and on reaching the door to his room, had even attempted to drag her inside. But he was so ridiculous she had laughed at him, pushed him away, given his crotch an unexpected little squeeze, and left him tottering outside the room at 2 a.m. with a drunken hangdog expression on his face.

The woman she now regarded in the mirror, had certainly

seen a bit of the world. She had five hundred Class A shares in Talsera, her original signing bonus, whose worth, while not giving her major voting power, now represented a respectable sum which had grown over the years. She also had some land in Goa and a nice Gurgaon apartment which was rented out for a small fortune. She now wore Gucci pumps and M&S suits, was driven around the city by a personal driver in her own luxury SUV, she owned the biggest baddest BlackBerry on the market, and used a gold iPod. Shivani peered at her grown-up body and face and at her stylish short haircut. A closet full of pretty French clothes awaited her, and so did the tiny bottle of Phensedyl she always kept in her handbag. Life was a party.

For the day's status review, she was planning to wear something tight, black and suggestive, something that would show him a lot of leg. She picked her outfit, doused herself with Lovely by Sarah Jessica Parker, and dressed in a hurry. She would need to confer with Ricky Talsera before the meeting, reassure him the client was happy and get his notes. Her BlackBerry beeped from the bureau top. It was an SMS from Ricky.

devries has cancelled the status review again. says tmrw. any idea what is going on?

Postponed? What the hell was that all about? Nothing had been said last night. Shivani narrowed her thick eyebrows, pursed her Ultra Rouge lips. Her thumbs flew over the keypad.

will find out right now. call you later

She immediately dialled DeVries's mobile phone. No answer. She called the Radisson switchboard, rang his room. No answer. Calm down, Shivani, she thought. He's probably in the shower, or

79

still asleep. Was he hiding something from me all evening? What the fuck is he up to?

Shivani called her driver and arranged to be at Radisson within half an hour. Her network of spies there would probably give her some answers. After that, she would head to the office for a face to face with Ricky. Before she left her flat, she logged onto her company email and found twenty forwards from different people, all with links to a particularly nasty blogpost. Of course she immediately read it. The blogger intimated something was wrong with *her*!

Could it get any more complicated? Jan DeVries had disappeared into the ether, and somebody was repeatedly trashing Talsera in general, her project specifically, and herself personally on the Internet. It could only be that little shit Vikram, she thought. She swore he would go down in flames if she found out he had anything to do with it. She opened the glassine envelope she kept in her makeup box, took a little pinch of the cocaine inside and sniffed it delicately, not a fat line like many of her club friends did.

Instantly she felt alive, awake, and ready to take control.

8

Nineteen across, four letters, a Presocratic philosopher. Khaneja's mind drifted back to his Philosophy classes at Stanford. Xeno of Elea, he remembered with satisfaction, filling in the letters in the boxes.

Ding! He looked up from his *International Herald Tribune* and caught sight of Jan DeVries exiting an elevator and striding through the Radisson Gurgaon lobby. He was dressed down—casual trousers, Lacoste polo, a plaid silk blazer, Italian suede loafers with interlocking buckles and Ray-Bans. That was interesting: DeVries normally wore suits and ties. Khaneja ducked down behind his newspaper, but kept an eye out. DeVries traded a few words at the reception desk and a red-turbaned Sikh hotel driver in white uniform approached him. The two men left by the front doors. Danny Khaneja waited until they were out of sight; then crept up to the bell captain and held out his hand. The man shook it and expertly palmed the five-hundred-rupee note he had concealed there.

"Karim's in Old Delhi," he whispered. "White Ambassador.

Number 2086. Surjit is driving." And he turned smartly to open the door of an arriving vehicle.

Well, well, Khaneja thought. Going sightseeing without telling us. See you there, asshole.

And he hurried to his car.

Shaitan Vikram took an auto-rickshaw to the Dwarka Sector 9 Metro Station and boarded the Metro from there. The ride to Rajiv Chowk, where he had to change trains, was long but it gave him time to review the situation, gloat a little too. It had been a particularly satisfying phone call with Jan DeVries earlier. He had cloaked his voice with a gizmo he had unearthed at Chatterjee Electricals in Nehru Place. Mr Chatterjee, deluged by a sea of electronics in his tiny shop, had no idea of the value of the second-hand scrambling device. Vikram had snapped it up for five hundred rupees, a fucking bargain for a miracle of engineering like that. Vikram's natural voice perched midway between squeaky and screechy. Using the device, he listened to himself as Darth Vader. That was entertaining, but not quite right. So he tried to mix in a little Robo-Cop. That sounded better. He dialed DeVries's number.

DeVries had immediately answered, "Hello?" He sounded disoriented as if he had been napping.

"Mr DeVries, this is your representative from KnightTuring."

"I wondered how you were going to pronounce that."

"KnightTuring," Vikram repeated forcefully. "There is a serious problem with the last release of the RoodInfo mobile app. It randomly overbills 10% of the transactions by 1.73%, a near-imperceptible distortion. You of course know it's already in production. Your current vendor didn't even suspect it or test for it. All you need for your meeting today is the leverage this knowledge brings you. You would be able to squeeze the team any way you like after you reveal this. Which brings us to our contract. As discussed, you must send my down payment of one thousand euros at your earliest convenience. Also, it's time we started some real business. But for that to happen, you must ditch the other guys. As soon as they are out of the picture, you and I can do some serious damage in the world together."

"So far this is all conjecture," DeVries replied. "I won't give money until the value of the information is proven."

Vikram snickered. It sounded like Robo-Cop catching a chest cold. "Karim's, near Jama Masjid," he said. "Be there at half past noon. Find the big restaurant, then turn right and go inside the little place on the left. Walk along the right side wall facing the kitchen, and then go up the stairs to this little dining area above. It's kind of stuffy, but not too bad. Occupy a table for two and order lamb kebab, and Pepsi if you want. Avoid the onions and the water of course. Wait for our representative. He will give you the information you need. Then you should be ready to do business." And he hung up.

Vikram looked up at the Blue Line map. Twelve more stops to Rajiv Chowk, where he would change, and then ride three more stops to Chandni Chowk. He wore a new pair of Diesel Jeans he had found at the Ambience Mall for ₹2000 and a new Ralph Lauren shirt. His glasses were SPY Optics. His shoes were grey leather Converse high tops, which, the salesman had assured him, looked "killer." A young woman in a parrot-green sari was seated next to him. She was reading a science textbook of some kind. Vikram snickered. The young woman got up and moved to another seat.

Vikram smiled. KnightTuring was about to strike again.

At that very moment, on the back seat of a white Ambassador snaking its way to Old Delhi, Jan DeVries sat, calculating. While he had little idea of where he was going, he somehow felt like a man in control. With the help of KnightTuring, he hoped to be able to manipulate Talsera. Cash was very tight at RoodInfo and he wanted to leverage every penny he could. If they were resistant or inept, he had the hungry newcomer ready to do business with. And if KnightTuring turned out to be worthless, he would, in any case, pressure Talsera for better pricing. It was, as the Americans often said, a win–win situation.

After he had been through all the scenarios, he looked out the window at the city, and was startled by the ragged skyline, the half-constructed office buildings, and the broad fields of mud and shacks, with the occasional satellite dish jutting up from the horizon. He marveled at the obvious energy of the place and the constant forward motion of its people. The car's interior was clean enough but every little depression and pothole in the road either rattled the vehicle or sent them flying. Even though the Sikh driver kept his mouth shut, the constant honking of horns continually unnerved him. He hoped that Karim's was a calm spot where he would be able to get a good look at the man KnightTuring was sending with the secret information. Life, DeVries remembered, was theatre. And so, on to the next act.

"What do you mean, Karim's?" Shivani nearly screamed at the deskman at the Radisson Gurgaon, leaning over so that her nose nearly touched the tip of his. The man nervously pushed back his comb-over and tried not to look at her bosom. His brilliant orange hairline was testimony to a recent *mehndi* dye job. But his roots were black. His manager had already spoken to him about it.

"Ma'am will please keep her voice down so as not to disturb the other guests," the man suggested meekly, looking around with real discomfort. Guests were staring; his manager was bound to hear about this. His life in the hospitality industry was over. He was never going to work in this town again. The thought that he should pack up and go live with his sister in Muradabad the same day, ran through his mind. Shivani resisted the urge to go ballistic.

"Karim's?" she repeated. "What the hell is he doing at Karim's?"

"Ma'am, that is guest's business."

"Call his driver right now."

"Mr DeVries does not carry a mobile?"

"Of course he carries a mobile!" Shivani said. "But I want to talk to the driver." The deskman couldn't follow the complicated logic of all this. He tried to remember what they had taught him in the Guest Relations course at the Krishna College of Hotel Management of Greater Bangalore, but there was nothing in his memory about the protocol of telephoning drivers to determine the whereabouts of guests. Shivani felt her temperature rising. She glared even more threateningly at the deskman, who shriveled further behind the counter. "Karim's," she said. "That's all you know?"

The deskman took out a crumpled handkerchief and mopped at his brow. "Yes, ma'am," he said. "That's all I know."

Shivani stormed out of the hotel and ordered her driver to take her to Chandni Chowk. She didn't know what she was going to find there, but she already didn't like it. She was aware they were about to stray into ugly congestion and that it would probably take her an hour to get to Jama Masjid.

After she left, the deskman popped two Crocins, called Danny Khaneja and told him everything that had transpired.

So Shivani has no clue either what her client is doing, Khaneja thought.

Khaneja was the first to reach Jama Masjid. He settled himself on the crowded steps of the masjid and waited among a throng of people. He didn't quite know what he was waiting for. DeVries was not going to get there for a while, Shivani much later. But he knew DeVries would pass by the steps on his way to Karim's, and he intended to pick him up from there.

It was mid-day and Old Delhi was teeming with people of all ages, colour and class. A persistent din pervaded the scene—hawkers yelling at vendors, ragpickers competing with curio sellers, cycle rickshaws and two-wheelers jostling for any empty space and beggars and street criminals chasing opportunity. Yet there was an implicit order in everything, secret systems which kept the wheels turning. Amidst all the chaos, colours, smells and the general sensory bombardment, Khaneja felt a familiarity that he had never known when living overseas. Just then, some steps below him, at the edge of the meandering crowd, something familiar caught his eye.

It was Shaitan Vikram. He was standing next to a trinkets seller, scoping out the territory outside Karim's. It was a transformed Vikram. He wore designer jeans, a branded business shirt and pricey shades. But still with a bad haircut and still easily distracted by his stomach. As if on cue, Shaitan Vikram looked at his watch and impulsively sat down in front of a chaat wallah and ordered two samosas.

Khaneja used the opportunity to slide unseen into the passageway that led to Karim's. He found a corner table in the big restaurant from where he could see everything and dialled Jaitendra's number.

"Guess who I just found," he said.

"Shaitan Vikram?" Jaitendra said.

"How did you . . . ?"

"Suresh. He's watching you right now, but you won't be able to see him. Shall I call him off?"

"Yes, do that. I'm at Karim's. How soon can you get here? I want you to take over Vikram."

"Ten minutes."

"Ten minutes? Okay, so Vikram belongs to you. I'll stay with DeVries. Oh, and The Destroyer is also coming to the party. But you of course already know this, don't you?"

"Correct," Jaitendra said.

9

One day earlier, 350 kilometres away, in a remote village in rural Rajasthan, two men had said goodbye to their families and had then set out on foot. They carried little luggage—a small cloth bag slung over the shoulder of the older man and a blue nylon gym duffel bag with a white Nike swoosh ported by the younger one. The men walked for two hours over hilly terrain, past a succession of rice fields, and around a small mountain to reach a major two-lane artery. They then walked to the spot where rural buses stopped. Since it was still some time before the bus to the Gangapur Train Station arrived, the two squatted by the roadside and waited.

The older man, a landholder named Raj Kumarji, was portly but not fat, and wore a white turban and an ancient grey kurta-pajama suit, over which he had added a tan pin-striped Jawaharlal jacket which was showing its age. He was fifty-two-years-old, his eyes seemed extra large for his face, magnified under the huge lenses of his generic plastic spectacle frames and his white beard was meticulously trimmed. He was accustomed to getting his way.

The younger man, his nephew named Mahesh, was known mostly for his ability to throw his weight around. He looked all of his eighteen years, an angry product of wasted ambition and brief education. He wore trousers whose cuffs bunched at his ankles, dusty sandals, and a Megadeth T-shirt. Around his shoulders was draped a faded paisley shawl. There were scabs and bruises on his face and forearms, evidences of a recent altercation. He did not look particularly dangerous, but he was. As they walked, the men did not speak.

Shaitan Vikram finished his samosas, smacked his lips and used his handkerchief to wipe his hands. He looked at his Swatch watch. Plenty of time for DeVries to appear. Vikram knew the European dude wouldn't dare venture into Old Delhi on foot. He looked at the samosa wallah. "Give me another one," he said.

Out at the vast entry to Old Delhi, cars jockeyed for parking, taxis and buses disgorged passengers bound for Jama Masjid and pedestrians gesticulated as they vociferously negotiated with rickshaw wallahs. It was a scene which afforded immense pleasure to Subinspector Shamsher Singh whose practiced eye knew where every potential profit was to be found. His life was uncomplicated. He needed only to keep Ajit Hooda, the top boss of Old Delhi, happy; stay on top of collections; and keep the traffic flowing.

It was a little after midday when Subinspector Singh identified a white Ambassador, in perfect repair and driven by a red-turbaned Sikh, entering the chaotic lot and cruising into a parking spot. The driver, after paying the parking wallah, helped a *firangi* exit the car. The richly dressed man consulted with the Sikh driver, who arranged a cycle-rickshaw for him. The *firangi* climbed uncomfortably on to its hard seat and the rickshaw wallah began the bone-rattling, start-and-stop ride into Old Delhi.

Subinspector Singh smiled contentedly at the man. He motioned to a disreputable creature lurking close by, Lateef, a small-time drug dealer and professional scam artist who was a fixture of the neighbourhood. Gaunt and compulsive, with a full head of jet black hair, he always seemed to be either twitching nervously or blinking his eyes while hunching his bony shoulders and giving forth with pathetic little whimpers and gulps. He had no permanent address, no friends, no future, his sole material presence in the universe being a large and badly scratched red suitcase, which moved from place to place, in a harmonious synchronicity with Lateef's erratic existence. Wherever the red suitcase lay, he lived. He slept in a succession of hovels, sometimes sharing a bed with a transsexual prostitute who took occasional pity on him. Lateef didn't particularly like being favoured by Subinspector Singh, but he couldn't refuse the man who held absolute power over his freedom. These days, Lateef dreamed mostly of methamphetamine and continuously plotted how to get his hands on more of it. The subinspector had of late, been an occasional and unlikely source for it. However, the supply from him always came at a price.

Lateef cowered as he shuffled over to Singh. He was careful neither to touch him, nor to disturb the impeccable crease of his shirt.

"*Haanji*, sahib?"

"You see that white man in the cycle-rickshaw there?" he asked, pointing his lathi in DeVries's direction.

"Yes. The gora, no?"

"Yes. I want you to help him in any way you can."

"Ah, I understand. I am to help him."

Subinspector Singh smiled. "Yes," he said. "Offer him things, whatever he needs." He pulled out a small plastic packet of white powder and handed it over to Lateef, who received it as if it was *prasad*. "If he doesn't want help, slip this into his jacket. Understand?"

Lateef nodded his assent, put the packet in his pocket and scurried off into the crowd, following the rickshaw. He had done this before for Subinspector Singh. He knew what was expected of him, and the consequences of not following orders. He would offer the man things.

From his position at the end of the passage outside Karim's, Danny Khaneja studied the tiny area which connected all three of Karim's different dining rooms. He knew there was a dining loft with a low ceiling off to the right.

Khaneja snapped the first picture with his cell phone when he saw a low-life bother Jan DeVries on his way into the narrow passage that led to Karim's. He seemed to be a very insistent beggar. Finding a cinematic quality in the scene, Khaneja switched over to the recording mode and zoomed in close, just in time to capture the beggar bumping the Dutchman and inserting a small white packet into his jacket pocket. DeVries disappeared hurriedly down the passageway and into the restaurant on the right. Khaneja made himself invisible and followed him discreetly through the passage, lingering off to the left of the doorway, behind a crowd milling about in front of the bread-bakers. DeVries went up to the dining loft, took a seat and gave an order. Khaneja snapped a photo. Held still.

Shaitan Vikram saw the street scum talk to DeVries. Where'd that guy come from? The beggar wouldn't let him alone, wouldn't let him pass by and kept talking to him until he got shoved out of the way. Served the loser right, Shaitan Vikram thought. He held back and watched DeVries go in. Unseen, Khaneja snapped another photo. Vikram stood alone for a while in the passage. Then he went in the same way the Dutch guy did. Khaneja saw him climb the narrow steps, then pick his way to the table and sit down across from DeVries. The two men instantly began to talk.

Khaneja moved to a table downstairs, just below the loft, sandwiching himself in between two diners. He could see the loft clearly, but among the throng and the noise and the patrons moving about, he remained unobserved by Vikram and DeVries. Khaneja took a series of pictures which neatly captured the clandestine episode—two men in costume playing roles, surrounded by working men, but oblivious of their surroundings, locked in their own conversation; one man passing a folded paper to the other; the other pocketing the paper.

It was 4 a.m., and chilly, when Raj Kumarji and his nephew arrived at the Gangapur City Train Station. There were still some hours for the train to Delhi to arrive. So, they made up their simple beds under a jacaranda tree at the end of the platform and fell fast asleep. By 7 a.m., when they got up, the place was a sea of humanity. It was announced that the Delhi train was two hours late. Raj Kumarji and Mahesh went back to sleep. They knew the train would eventually arrive and that Raj Kumarji would find a place in an unreserved coach. Four hours later they would be in Delhi.

Years earlier, Subinspector Singh had learned a very useful English phrase. He had arrested a twenty-something American tourist purchasing bhang from a small-time dealer. The tourist didn't recognise that Singh was actually doing him a favour. The dealer was a rough character with a bad reputation. The kid was better off with the police. So, he cuffed the young man, took him down to the station, put him in an interrogation room, gave him time to get nervous and then questioned him severely. Did he understand the seriousness of the charges against him? Yes, he did. Was he aware that the Indian courts could put him away for years, simply for possession of the illegal substance? Yes, he was aware of it. Did he also know that he may have to stay in jail for years, even before his case was heard? Yes. And did he need to tell the young man the usual procedure for this kind of offence? No, it was not necessary; he would cooperate. Subinspector Singh searched the young man's wallet, discovered he came from Oak Park, Illinois, and had $250 in cash, two ATM cards and several thousand rupees.

"I can suggest an alternative to the usual judicial process," he told the young man. "Just pay me a fine of $250 right now."

What the young man replied, Subinspector Singh could not at first understand. He had used a term which Singh had never heard before. However, once it was explained to him, he found it a very useful linguistic flourish, and he remembered it at the oddest moments. Like minutes earlier when he had surreptitiously watched the geek and the European sit down together across a table at Karim's. He knew he had to choose between pursuing one of the two. It was another of those instances when he again recalled what the American had said to him years before: "Well, if you ask me, it's a *no-brainer*."

Jaitendra stared hungrily at the mutton *burra* kebabs which sat before Khaneja. "Those look good," he said. "The paratha looks good too." He had just slipped into the seat across from Khaneja. It amazed Khaneja how effortlessly Jaitendra could move about, unnoticed.

"The food just arrived," Khaneja said. "Oh, Vikram's getting ready to move." He nodded towards the loft.

"Yes. I can see him."

"Jaitendra, there's no time to enjoy the kebabs. We can come back another day."

Jaitendra tore off a piece of bread, pinched at a kebab and stuffed it into his mouth. "*Mrr crdvat*?" he asked, chewing happily.

"I don't get you."

"Your drink?" Jaitendra said, pointing at a full cup in the middle of the table. Khaneja shook his head no, and shrugged. Jaitendra grabbed it and took a long pull off it, then made himself another kebab and bread and stuffed it into his mouth. Looked up. "He is moving. I'll talk to you later." He took one more long draught from the cup and evaporated.

The man sitting next to Khaneja turned around and reached for his drink. He raised it to his lips and hesitated, looked inside the rim. "Hey," he said, "my cup's half full. Somebody drank half my sherbet." He turned in all directions, looking for the culprit. Khaneja pretended disbelief, then ignorance. He could see the loft above the man's head. DeVries and Vikram got up but did not shake hands. Vikram hurried away first, never looking back. Jan DeVries, clearly disoriented, prepared to leave too. Khaneja's cue: he darted outside, back to the crowd in front of the bread-bakers, hanging back across from the restaurant door. Out at the entrance to the passage, he caught a glimpse of Subinspector Singh handcuffing the beggar who had earlier accosted DeVries and attaching him to an iron grate where the passage faced the alley. His camera went click. He watched DeVries carefully pick his way down the narrow stairs and out to the passage, and then turn left. The guy looked lost in thought. Khaneja gave him half a minute, then followed discreetly. But as soon as he rounded the corner, he again held back. Silhouetted at the far end of the passage stood the unmistakable figure of Subinspector Shamsher Singh. And he appeared to be caught up in a tense conversation with Jan DeVries. Khaneja's camera went click. For the moment, he decided to stay with the policeman, who was now in possession of DeVries anyway.

10

As he stood before the police officer in the passage, Jan Devries remembered how strange it had all seemed from the beginning, how he had felt all along that invisible signals were being exchanged on all sides. The odd dialogue between the driver and the parking monitor; the strange dealing with the rickshaw wallah; and, most surprisingly, the beggar who had accosted him with a succession of offers in surprisingly clear English. He had had to refuse [in order] a tour, naughty porn, a girl, hashish, bhang, coke, two girls, boys and finally virgins. Exasperated, he had had to shove the man out of his way.

All the more irksome had been the meeting with the agent from KnightTuring. They'd sent some amateur messenger boy in stretch jeans who treated the whole thing like it was a Matt Damon movie. He sat down without a greeting and then immediately began to outline, in his difficult-to-understand accent, three new areas of vulnerability in the RoodInfo application. It took DeVries a moment to recognise that the man was speaking in English.

After handing him a folded paper containing essential

information, he said, "That's all for now." After this, he hurriedly stood up, didn't even shake hands, and got the hell out of Karim's, even before the Dutchman could say bye. As DeVries stood there alone, he gradually became aware of his isolation and his vulnerability in the surroundings. Big moustached men talked loudly around him and the air in the loft hung thick with swirling unfamiliar aromas of breads and curries. The noise level was deafening. Nobody was speaking English. He must get out of this place quickly, head back to the Radisson and then deal with Talsera.

Was the messenger boy playing dumb? Did he know more than he let on? Maybe. Was he one of the geniuses KnightTuring claimed they had? Jesus Christ, DeVries thought, what if that kid is the *only* genius?

But when he had stood up from the table, threaded his way downstairs and out through the crowded doorway and started walking towards the end of the passage, a uniformed police officer had stepped in front of him, the man who now blocked his exit.

At the Chandni Chowk Metro Station, Shaitan Vikram leapt aboard the train towards Rajiv Chowk. Jaitendra stayed behind him, unseen from the next car, observing his every move. Vikram plugged in his iPod Nano, closed his eyes and retreated into his own world. His right knee did a little bop in place as he nervously jiggled his heel up and down to no apparent rhythm. With a little luck, Jaitendra thought, he will lead me to his new workplace where I may get to do some serious digging.

"Hello, Khaneja? Narayan here. How come you never answer

your phone? I received your text about a donation for that South Indian temple. Man, so many other people also asking me for Diwali donations these days. What, you think I am made of money? Call me up when you can. By the way, you're staying out of trouble, right? Hahahaha. Honestly, you need to get out and have some fun, man, good, clean fun! You work too hard. Listen, I'll talk to you later. I booked a tummy tuck in fifteen minutes. I'll try you after dinner. I want to hear if my stitches are holding up on you. Hahahaha."

Raj Kumarji got aboard the unreserved second class coach and found a compartment with some vacant space between an old man and a large woman in a pink sari. Outside, chai wallahs walked up and down the length of the train, halting at windows, dispensing scalding hot chai as indigent children scurried around the car wheels, waiting for trash to fall. The woman in the pink sari on Raj Kumarji's left, brought out an elaborate system of containers of food which she began to assemble and hand around. The old man on his right nodded off and rested his head on Raj Kumarji's shoulder.

Mahesh could be observed outside to the right of the compartment door. He was already smoking cigarettes with some other men of his age, half of them hanging out of the windows and staring at women. The boy would come to no good, Raj Kumarji reflected. He had not succeeded in school and could not join the family business. He could not be sent to an ashram. No rich family would marry their daughter to him. He is only good for one thing, fighting, and that is why I have brought him along.

If he needed to put some pressure, the boy would serve. He would do as he was told. Raj Kumarji sincerely hoped the boy would not be needed, but it was better to have him to make a point. He looked around the crumbling train compartment, leaned his head against the old man's and was instantly asleep.

Shivani seethed. She glowered as the car moved slowly and imperceptibly through endless lanes of traffic. She was boxed in by vehicles on all sides, caught between the looming wall of a rusted bus and a behemoth yellow lorry, marooned in a sea of "Horn Please" trucks, two-wheelers buzzing by and cars everywhere else. She was a prisoner within her steel and glass fortress, confined in a climate-controlled, air-filtered and soundproofed prison on wheels. The car inched ahead. Stopped. Lurched forward. Halted abruptly. Frozen in time, the honking seemed to increase, and she felt she might remain stuck there forever. The horn-honking doubled. At this rate she would get to Karim's only by dinner time. And DeVries wasn't taking her calls. She had even left him messages at the Radisson, SMSed him, emailed him. But nothing, no reply.

Woe to the ragged girl who stopped by the car window at that moment and tap-tap-tapped. She was rather hungry, but she needed to do another hour of begging before they would let her go and play. She was thinking of a sweet, and she was thirsty. She stared into the face of the rich woman behind the glass, a woman who looked like a movie star with bright red lips and eyes heavily made-up, and brought her finger tips together to point them at her mouth as she had been taught. For this, she received a look of venom, a dark, intense and angry glare. She fled. Shivani burned. The car did not move.

Alone in his Gurgaon office in Building 2, Ricky Talsera stared blankly at the white board facing his desk. He needed to look closely at the numbers and figures scribbled on it, but he couldn't get himself interested. Ricky looked across inside the glass cabinet that had stacks of unread scientific journals, an array of trophies and awards commemorating triumphs long forgotten, t-shirts folded neatly into an orderly stack by Miss Briganza, artifacts and souvenirs handed over at competitors' trade show booths and imprinted memo pads he hated to use because they said "Ricky Talsera, Founder" on them. He was tired of giving away the usual swag. He wondered whether those objects even helped people remember Talsera at all.

Ricky shifted his attention back to the white board but still couldn't focus. There was too much going on. DeVries had gone to Jama Masjid, and not for sightseeing—this much he knew from Khaneja's and Jaitendra's calls. Another nasty blogpost had just appeared. Shaitan Vikram had resurfaced and seemed to be up to no good. The RoodInfo status review meeting's schedule was again uncertain. The Destroyer hadn't called in yet, for which he was infinitely grateful, though she was supposed to be keeping tabs on her client. It would be interesting to hear *her* explanations of what was afoot, he thought. Did she even know? And then there was the customary silence from Rajan Abraham: off somewhere with his team of nerds, coding some proof-of-concept using a new technology and trying to catch the hacker. Ricky would call them all in for a meeting later that day. His minimalist office was significantly larger in floor space than the first apartment he had ever rented. His office had four panes of tall windows overlooking trees, some construction visible, some open space and even some sky. People liked to meet here because there was so much daylight. His desk was an ocean of bleached, blond wood and three rolling chairs stood in place, side by side, facing Ricky's chair, spanning the length of the desk. Everything (bless Briganza!) was in order: whiteboard markers kept neatly in the pen stand, the temperature controller aligned with the mobile phone and with the handset which dimmed the room lights, the wireless mouse in its place, the wireless keyboard clean and dusted, the calculator ready to use, the phone and its teleconferencing docking station all well arranged.

Ricky ignored the white board. He picked up his mobile phone and called up Shaalu. She answered on the first ring.

"How unusual to hear from you at midday!" she said, clearly pleased.

"I was just thinking about you. Umm, I guess I just wanted to tell you how much I love you, that's all . . ."

Shaalu laughed. "Love you too. But I don't think I can stay on the phone for long right now. Too much going on with the kids."

"I just needed to hear your voice."

"I'll see you tonight, honey. We will switch off the phones and turn on the red light bulb."

"Now you're talking," Ricky said.

Outside his office door Priyanka waited. Ricky had asked her to investigate Pushpa's problem with the dog and she was ready to report. She consulted her wristwatch—three minutes to go before their appointment. His door was closed. Miss Briganza was nowhere to be seen. As happened quite frequently when she was waiting to meet Ricky, a movie which she had seen many years ago came back into her mind.

The movie took place in a typical Indian village. It began with the main character, a young doctor, strolling through town, saying good morning to those he met. He was obviously greatly respected. He sang a song which compared people to rays of sunshine. He had a wife who was very sick. In a series of flashbacks, the film told the story of their courtship, struggle and marriage. A group of lovable secondary characters added to the tale which had many moments of great happiness and occasional sadness. Priyanka liked that part the most where the doctor stopped at a shop every Friday after work, to take home his wife's favourite sweets. A girl who worked in the shop's kitchen secretly fell in love with him, but she was betrothed to a man whom she did not particularly like. The girl eventually agreed to a loveless marriage, and her husband soon showed himself to be a cad. Meanwhile, the doctor's wife grew weaker and weaker. The doctor sang a poignant song which asked if the sun ever dims in the sky, while the girl from the sweet shop sang her own lament, overlapping his, asking why love never came to her.

The doctor's wife eventually died. The girl's unfaithful husband disappeared. She and the doctor started a chaste friendship but of course, the townspeople misunderstood it. Then one day, her husband came back. He confided to the doctor that he had a rare disease, and begged the doctor to not tell his wife about it. He later reformed and became best friends with the doctor. Then he died.

One Friday the doctor passed by the sweet shop and impulsively decided to go in. The girl from the kitchen and the doctor realised they were in love, and the film ended with them singing about every day bringing a new sunrise. The film was called *Raastey ka Gulab*.

11

The basement canteen quickly cleared after the bustling lunch hour. Only a single couple remained, seated across from each other, at a table along the right-hand wall. The young woman wore a long orange kurta with a blue churidar, and a modest peacock green dupatta. The boy seated opposite her wore faded blue jeans and a grey T-shirt with the word "Hero" printed on it. They wished they could touch fingertips, but such a display would encourage office gossip and cause them trouble. The girl wished they had a secret place to go where she could simply lean into his chest as she loved to do, and place her ear to his heart, his strong arms wrapped around her.

"I'm sure the letter must have reached him by now," Adita said. "But he still hasn't called. I am afraid of what it means. It's not like him to go silent."

"Perhaps he is considering giving us his blessing."

"Ravi, the probability of that happening is nearly zero. You don't know my father. I am sure he will disown me. He will forbid me to come home ever again. I will lose my family." Adita bowed her head and held back the tears. "I should never have written. I wish I had gone home and told him in person. It would have been so much easier if ma was still alive."

"My family will protect you now," Ravi said.

Adita looked up at him abruptly. "I want the blessing of my family too, Ravi." And she turned her face away.

Hari Bhaiyya watched the young couple from behind the counter. He did not need to hear their words to understand. She had told her father, and the news was not good.

The twitching little man who had approached DeVries on the way in, stood in the shadows off to the left. He had been handcuffed to a metal grate which covered the window of an old building. He faced the wall, his arms elevated just to the point of discomfort and twisted around. He blinked his eyes repeatedly and was hyperventilating.

The police officer still blocked Jan DeVries's passage. Impeccably barbered, freshly pressed uniform. Name badge reading SINGH pinned to the left breast pocket of his starched khaki shirt. Nice boots, shined to mirror finish. And a very beautiful silver-tipped stick. He wore a revolver in a reddish-brown leather holster at his hip, snapped shut. He was smiling.

"Sir will kindly answer a few questions," the policeman said matter-of-factly, not moving out of the way. He nodded in the direction of Lateef and continued, "This man here has made serious accusations against you." Lateef began to babble in Hindi about not knowing anything at all. "Shut up," the policeman said, and Lateef went silent. "I will need to examine your visa."

"My visa?" DeVries knew he was not carrying his passport. "What accusations?"

Subinspector Singh stared angrily at Lateef. "Tell Sir what he asked you for."

"Drugs!" Lateef cried. "Sir asked me for white powder!"

"Now just one moment . . ." DeVries attempted, but Lateef's bellow interrupted him.

"I am telling the truth, I swear! Look in jacket pocket! White powder is in jacket pocket!"

"Be quiet, both of you!" Singh barked and turned his attention to DeVries. "Did you ask this man for hard drugs?"

"I don't know what your game is," DeVries said. "But this is preposterous. The man offered me drugs and a host of other illegal things, but I, of course, refused. He wouldn't leave me alone and I finally had to push him out of my way."

"Sir is a tourist?" Singh asked, though he knew DeVries was not one. "Your passport, please? I will first examine your tourist visa."

"Sir asked me for white powder!" Lateef repeated, struggling with the cuffs which scraped against the metal grate just above his head. His hands were beginning to grow white and numb. He had been through this kind of performance before. He knew what was expected of him.

"I told you to keep quiet!" Singh struck Lateef sharply on his forehead with the stick and Lateef shut up. He would have a respectable bump there tonight. "And, sir, you will need to cooperate. This is official police investigation."

DeVries figured he better get Shivani or Danny Khaneja on

the phone, and quick. He reached towards his lapel in the direction of his mobile phone. Subinspector Singh instantly reacted. "Sir will please keep his hands at his sides. In plain sight."

"Now you look here," Jan DeVries said. "I didn't ask this imbecile for anything. He offered me every commodity he could think of. I'm the one being set up!"

"So you accuse this man of soliciting?"

"If that's what you want to call it."

"If Sir will not cooperate and answer questions directly, then investigation will need to move to police *thana*. Do you understand?"

Lateef heard the word *thana* repeated and began to dance about, twisting right and left. He knew his cue, but he dreaded spending another night in the cells, which sometimes happened when he helped Subinspector Singh. He dreamed of the methamphetamine Subinspector Singh could provide later. "Sir has taken package of white powder from me and not paid me!" he said.

"This man says you stole drugs from him."

"Why would I do that?" DeVries said. "Steal drugs from a street person? Ridiculous."

"I will be asking the questions," Singh said. "Did you or did you not receive drugs from this man?"

"Of course I did not!" DeVries said. "You think I'd come to a place like this for drugs?"

"Passport, please," Subinspector Shamsher Singh said, holding out his hand. He tapped the ground impatiently with the stick he held in his other hand. "I will first need to establish your identity."

"My passport is in my room at the Radisson Gurgaon, you fool," DeVries stammered. "I don't walk around places like these with official documents in my pocket."

"Since you refuse to cooperate, we will take the investigation to police *thana* right away to establish your identity and file the necessary reports. I will take your statement." He produced a mean-looking set of handcuffs. "Please turn around and cross your wrists behind your back."

DeVries looked hard at the man. "You've got to be kidding," he said. "I can have *you* arrested for this. I've done nothing wrong."

"Sir will please turn around and cross his wrists." Singh repeated. He blew a police whistle and a constable came running down the lane towards them. "Please do not resist arrest," he said to the Dutchman. DeVries scowled, but slowly turned around, and felt the metal bracelets bind his wrists tightly. He was ready to throw whatever sum of money was needed to get him off the hook. The constable took his arm, and turned him around again, admiring the soft touch of the Italian silk fabric of DeVries's jacket. "We will now walk to the *thana*," Singh said.

"I'll make certain you lose your badge over this," DeVries growled. "Mark my words."

"Perhaps," the Subinspector said. "Or perhaps we will work out a satisfactory arrangement. This way, please."

Khaneja had made himself invisible again. He had watched the whole interaction between Subinspector Singh and DeVries and clicked occasional pictures. He had seen this kind of thing before. It never did any good to lose one's cool with the police. Instead, one must remain flexible and cooperate and go along with the flow of events. DeVries's natural arrogance had only made it worse for him.

Khaneja regarded these developments as advantageous for Talsera. If Jan DeVries was kept out of circulation at the police *thana* for the rest of the day, it would give them more time to check out what Shaitan Vikram was up to. He knew that the policeman would place DeVries in a holding room for several hours to soften him up, and would then try and cut a deal. He watched as the procession of men left the passage—the inspector in the lead, followed by a handcuffed DeVries, then Lateef, also handcuffed, and finally the constable, shoving Lateef theatrically. As soon as they disappeared down the lane, Khaneja texted Jaitendra.

I am staying here. Client arrested. Will advise. Calling Ricky now.

Jaitendra received the SMS outside an Internet café where it looked like Vikram had dropped in to post anonymously on some message boards. He texted Khaneja back.

V at internet café. May get a chance to visit his apartment while he's busy.

Priyanka consulted her digital watch: 2:59:30. She inhaled deeply, prepared to knock on Ricky's office door precisely at the scheduled moment. It had been some time since she had last met Ricky alone. Priyanka knew she was jealous of Shaalu, of how successfully she kept Ricky happy. But if he ever needed her, if something ever happened to Shaalu, she would make herself available. She would reveal to him the love and admiration she felt for him. She too could make him happy. She straightened the lapels on her jacket and rapped on the door three times.

"Just a moment, Priyanka," Ricky said through the closed door. His mobile was ringing. Khaneja calling.

The red-turbaned Sikh had taken the previous day off for a festival and had spent all of it at a gurdwara. He had stayed there late into the night, singing. This morning he had reported late for work at Radisson Gurgaon. The deskman had told him that a Dutchman had booked him for the entire day. After eating his breakfast with the other drivers at the long table in the small and windowless dining-room off the kitchen, he had meticulously wiped down the exteriors of his white Ambassador and had scrutinised every corner of its interior. After that, he had reassembled the marigolds which garlanded his guru's portrait on the dashboard, listened to a radio program, spoken to his wife on the mobile phone and was halfway through listening to a recorded sermon on his iPod clone when the desk called for him. His client was in a great hurry to get to Jama Masjid. Not a very polite gentleman. He had used whatever shortcuts he knew to reach the destination as quickly as possible. Then he had put the disagreeable man into a cycle-rickshaw headed for Karim's and prepared to wait some more.

The man had said he would be no more than an hour. Plenty

of time for a midday nap. So, he set his phone to vibrate, reclined the front seat of his taxi, closed his eyes and quickly fell fast asleep.

Dr Narayan sat at his desk in his wood-panelled office, leaned back in his red leather upholstered chair, took a sip of his midday whisky and thought about Danny Khaneja. He owed Khaneja many favours. It was never clear how he had first reached him—typical of Khaneja, he always knew the right person to call at the right time. These were the conditions under which their acquaintance had begun five years ago.

That night the phone awoke the doctor at 2 a.m. The caller mentioned the name of a senior politician, to whom Dr Narayan was obliged. Of course the doctor immediately agreed to meet him at his clinic, off Connaught Place, in half an hour.

Narayan, a punctilious man known for his dapper suits, stood only 5'3" tall and had the delicate hands required for reconstructive surgery. He had built his practice in Delhi catering to rich socialites, and was a sought-after guest at the best dinner tables. He had sculpted noses of the famous, reduced and enlarged bosoms of the powerful, improved chins and ears of the influential and had performed liposuction on more stomachs, thighs and posteriors of the anonymous rich than he could count. He was an irrepressibly cheerful man whose patients adored him. Once a year he returned to his ancestral village in the low Himalayas, where for two weeks he donated his time pro bono to the care of the poor locals.

When Narayan saw Khaneja standing outside his clinic under the bare street lights that first night, he was amazed the man was able to walk on his own. Khaneja wore what was once a well-tailored Brooks Brothers khaki suit, but it was clear he had been badly roughed up—pockets torn, seams ripped, a clean knife cut down one sleeve, stains and smudges, a trail of blood leading from the left ear to the chest. He inventoried the man's wounds and his mind began to work: Obviously an orbital blowout fracture typical from a punch in the face. You can see the eye socket pushed inward, fracture of the zygomatic arch, needs to be reduced. Lots of ice and anti-inflammatories. Those superficial skin lacerations would need some stitches. Hands badly bruised. Clean the wounds, should be fine. Surgical reattachment of the left ear necessary as soon as possible.

"Want to tell me what happened?"

"Can we deal with all that after you have done your repair, doc?" Khaneja said. He grimaced as he stepped through the doorway, half bent over.

"Abdominal trauma?" Narayan asked.

"I don't think so. I got kicked, it hurts, but everything seems to be functioning alright."

"You allergic to anything?"

"Small talk," Khaneja said, sitting down on the examination table and grunting.

"So what's the story? Who did this to you?" Narayan shined a light on his patient's face and began to clean the wounds. Khaneja winced. The doctor gave him a quick injection. "For pain," he muttered.

"Bar fight. A Nigerian."

"This may hurt, looks like you have a piece of glass in here. Ready?"

Khaneja nodded, held still. The doctor pulled a shard out of his right cheek. Khaneja exhaled audibly as it clinked in the small dish at the doctor's elbow. Dr. Narayan produced an oxygen mask. "Take this and inhale," he said. "I'll give you a mild tranquiliser in the meantime. You're in pretty bad shape, hahaha. What happened to the Nigerian?"

"Maybe his friends dragged him out. I don't know," Khaneja said. The oxygen helped. Soon he felt the immediate warmth of the anaesthetic all over his body. "It started over a joke about a scam."

"Tell me the joke."

"It was not funny,"

"Obviously not, hahahaha." He worked on Khaneja for almost three hours. The doctor leaned back in his expensive chair and swiveled around to look out at the verdant courtyard outside his office. He was always glad to hear from Khaneja. His unique skills in contract negotiation, business strategy and political introductions had benefitted him significantly in the last couple of years. His message just mentioned that he wanted a contribution for a South Indian temple. But you never knew with Danny Khaneja. He hoped this didn't somehow involve another Nigerian!

A thousand pairs of eyes followed Jan DeVries as he marched along the crowded lane in the direction of the Jama Masjid police *thana*. It was not the first time DeVries had been cuffed. The first time was at a soccer match when he was seventeen. He was out the next morning. Another time, a scorned lover had falsely accused him of assault and two Amsterdam detectives had taken him in. His father had intervened. Once, a wild party in Bangkok had been raided. The police were quite efficient about it all and quoted a bribe straight away. He was out of those cuffs in minutes. But *this* was different.

He was humiliated. His important business had been interrupted by some small-time cop. He glared at Singh walking in front of him. The man seemed to be known in the district. As he paraded his capture, he exchanged pleasantries with the local shopkeepers, who all seemed to fear him. This wasn't the first time they were witnessing such a performance. Nothing remarkable, just another walk to the station, then some squeezing and finally the inevitable payment.

"Through the doorway, please, smartly," Subinspector Singh said to DeVries as they reached the station.

Four thousand miles away, the fat Berthe opened her eyes and tried to clear her head of the usual early-morning cobwebs, residue of last night's alcoholic haze. It took her time to ascertain where she was—her own bedroom in her own opulent brick-and-slate house in the emerald countryside outside Rotterdam. On the curved cobblestone driveway in front of the house sat her perfectly restored Jaguar XJ12 sedan, parked next to Jan's new silver blue Bentley roadster. She had a gardener tending to the lilies, tulips and crocus and a full-time maid who already had a fire going in the salon and now sat chain-smoking in the kitchen, waiting for Berthe to ring for breakfast. It would be the same breakfast as every morning: one boiled egg, a slice of cheese, some local bread, confiture and a pot of *cafe au lait*, everything delivered on a silver tray set with fine china and linen, accented by a tea rose in a tiny

Delft vase. She scanned the room, her eyes crusted and stinging. Faint daylight bathed the walls, illuminating the gauze curtains that damped an already diffused sky. Something was wrong.

The fact that she had passed another night alone in bed did not trouble her. Jan was always away, and they had not had an intimate life for years now. Where was he travelling to this week? India? Yes, India. She suspected he had a mistress in Brussels, but they never spoke about that. For years she had detected suspicious scents of miscellaneous perfumes on his shirts following his business trips. On the rare occasions when he took her along, she had observed how he behaved with the stewardesses. Solicitous, jovial, flattering. Exactly the opposite of how he treated her.

She knew she was no longer the slender young thing he had married. She was now a fat, middle-aged provincial housewife, and probably a drunk. But, it wasn't her fault. Who would not have turned into such a burnt-out case, left to waste away alone, miles from civilisation, as she had been living for more than two decades? Once she had had a lover, an older aristocratic gentleman, but he had died years ago. She still missed their breathless Thursday afternoon assignations. She had not had the heart to seek out another man after him; who would anyway be attracted to her now that she looked like this? She would see out her days with Jan, living a desolate life amidst all the luxury.

Even the company of her women friends had grown tiresome. All they talked about was grandchildren, or how much they hated their husbands. Berthe did not hate Jan; he had kept his affairs away from her and from public view.

He was anyway unlike other husbands—he still paid all the

bills without a word and telephoned her every morning when he was on the road, no matter in which part of the world he was. Her life revolved around those calls. How pathetic, she thought, the big event of her day was a three-sentence conversation with a man she no longer cared about, and who no longer cared for her.

She remembered her engraved silver martini shaker. Today she would wait until 11 a.m. before mixing her first drink. The eerie sense that something was wrong still possessed her, but she could not tell what it was. She rang the bell for the maid. Minutes later her breakfast tray arrived.

"Madame has slept late this morning," the maid attempted. "Madame is feeling unwell?"

Berthe looked at the clock: 9.30 a.m. She immediately knew what was wrong: Jan unfailingly called at eight every morning, and today he was an hour and a half late. Probably a case of jet lag, she thought. He would eventually call. She spread confiture on her bread and dreamed of the martini shaker.

Overheated, a thin grimy film of sweat covering her body, Shivani stormed down the lane towards Karim's. She was determined to confront DeVries and find out what he was up to. Instead, to her surprise, she saw Danny Khaneja walking towards her.

"You!" she said. "What are *you* doing here?"

"Calm down, Shiv," Khaneja said. "There's stuff going on."

"What do you mean stuff? What kind of stuff? Why haven't I been told anything?"

Shivani could intimidate almost everyone at Talsera, but not Danny Khaneja. "Things have been happening pretty fast," he said. "Relax. By the way, you need to call the office at once and cancel the status review for today. Put it on hold indefinitely. Say anything, lie, invent a reason, I don't care."

"What are you talking about?" Shivani nearly screamed. "Where's Jan DeVries? He's supposed to be in Karim's."

"He was," Khaneja said. "Not there any longer."

"So where's he now?"

"At the Jama Masjid police *thana*."

"My God, I need to get over there right away. What else do you know?"

"You better stay away, Shiv. And by the way, there's more. Shaitan Vikram is back to haunt us. He seems to be the one behind those nasty blogposts."

Shivani stared at him, said nothing.

"And it appears he's been conspiring with Jan DeVries."

"Goddammit, I'm going over to the police station right now," Shivani said. "I'll get to the bottom of this."

"You will not. You're going to call the office and cancel the meeting and then you will go back and wait for my call."

He's not telling me the whole thing, Shivani thought. "I suppose your friend Jaitendra is involved?"

"No comments," Khaneja said. "At the moment I am keeping an eye on Mr DeVries. Your presence is not needed. In fact, you will only get in the way."

"What's he doing in the *thana*?" she said.

"He's in custody," Khaneja said. "Led away in handcuffs. I figure they're booking him now. I'll give them a couple of hours to do the paperwork, then get personally involved. Just go, Shiv.

Nothing's gonna happen for a long time. Go back to Gurgaon and wait for my call."

"You listen to me," she said, arms akimbo, steaming in the afternoon sun. "You screw this up, and then see how I get even. I will make you and your dashing war hero friend sorry you ever got involved. Is that clear enough? Do I need to make it any clearer?"

13

Ricky Talsera hit the green button on his iPhone. "Yes, Danny?"

"Man, you will not believe what is going on," Khaneja said.

"Surprise me. I could use some excitement."

"Shaitan Vikram just met DeVries at Karim's."

"I knew it," Ricky said. "He's definitely coaching our client against us. I must report this to the police immediately."

"Don't do anything yet. There's more."

"What else?" Ricky said.

"Wait, I am telling you the entire story. So, Jaitendra's following Vikram, and we should have some more information on that front soon. Their meeting at Karim's broke up half an hour ago. I took a few pictures with my phone. Vikram passed DeVries some document. Must be incriminating stuff and certainly useful to us. Oh and you won't believe what happened next."

"What? Please tell me."

"He just got busted."

"Busted? Did you say DeVries got busted?"

"A local cop planted some drugs on him. Luckily, I got it on film."

"Danny, you are amazing."

"I'll use the film to our best advantage at the right moment. For now, let's allow him to get settled in at the *thana*."

"Is there someone you can call?"

"Plenty of people. I know the local DCP, a contact of my Dad's. But I am not calling him now. I know how these things work. They'll hold DeVries in lockup for a couple of hours, which will actually help us out. It'll keep DeVries out of circulation until we get to the bottom of all this. Any word on who's reading our email and posting that stuff on the net?"

"Nothing yet," Ricky said. "Rajan says one of his boys is working on it."

"Okay, I'll stand by. And I have one more thing to tell you."

"My God, what else?"

"The Destroyer is nosing around. Showed up here at Jama Masjid. But I kept her away from the police and sent her back to the office, so get ready. I told her to cancel the status update indefinitely or at least until we get a handle on what's going on. It'll be interesting to see how she spins all this to her own advantage. I'll bet you a thousand she's been in touch with DeVries in the last two days."

"Before the status review? She's supposed to have told us."

"Right, right. If she hadn't been with us for so long or brought in so much business, I'd have suggested we get rid of her right away. I must disconnect now. I need to call Dad and have him phone Ajit Hooda."

"Your Dad knows Ajit Hooda?"

"Yes, old cricket buddies. Okay, listen Ricky, I gotta go. I'll call you as soon as I have more to report."

"What do I do about Shivani?"

"Just listen to her, nod appreciatively and offer her a cup of tea. Have Briganza interrupt you after a few minutes and tell Shivani you need to excuse yourself and take a call. Then hide out."

"What about—"

"Ricky, I really gotta go. Later, man."

Khaneja hung up abruptly. Ricky called Briganza and told her to have Hari Bhaiyya inform her as soon as Shivani showed up, and to interrupt their meeting after five minutes. Briganza said, "No problem, sir," and hung up. Suddenly, the contracts for the new campus seemed very interesting to Ricky and he reached for the fat document on the corner of his desk and began to read. Priyanka waited outside.

Unperturbed by the chaos, Raj Kumarji and Mahesh exited the train and shuffled along the platform, catching themselves in the ebb and flow of the crowd. They wove their way around cases and parcels and squatting families, around magazine stands and chai wallahs, past carts laden with bundles and suitcases and coolies with stacks of suitcases and bags balanced on their heads. Slowly, the two men climbed a crowded metal staircase which led to an overpass where they joined the creeping throng. Then they crossed over to another staircase which led down into a lobby thick with travellers drifting in all directions, and from there they threaded their way down to the row of open doors which led to the main crossing of the station where more human beings milled about. Here, Raj Kumarji motioned to his nephew to halt, and he himself stood still too, listening to the mélange of sounds which surrounded him. Finally he heard what he sought and looked towards the source of the voice.

"Gurgaon!" a man cried in as loud a voice as he could muster. "Gurgaon!" he shouted in each direction he turned, occasionally exchanging a few words with people who approached him. Some he directed to stand to the side and wait, others he dismissively sent on their way. This man was named Pyarelal. Six days a week he repeated this identical performance, in Gurgaon in the morning, then at the train station in the afternoon. First thing in the day, he went to the garage of Singh Transport, just off Connaught Place, a business owned by his cousin's uncle's cousin. There he was assigned a Toyota Qualis with an official capacity for six passengers. He next picked up six call-centre workers along a prescribed route, then dropped them at their office in Gurgaon. Once his car was empty he went straight to a staging spot for local taxis and siphoned off four litres of diesel into a row of one-litre plastic bottles, which he then sold to a regular group of taxi drivers. He had a cadre of loyal customers who supplied him with their extra empty bottles and as they stopped by the parked SUV for their fuel, they always chatted amiably. Then he went to the main crossing in Gurgaon, stood on the corner among other drivers and yelled "Nayi Delhi Railway Station! Railway Station!" After picking up as many people as he could, He shuttled to the station, got rid of them and looked for a new group to load. This was the point where Raj Kumarji intercepted him. His daily system was to be back in Gurgaon in time for his evening run in the opposite direction to carry the call-centre employees back home. At the end of the day, he went to deposit the car back to the lot near

Connaught Place. On a good day he took home an extra ₹500.

Raj Kumarji sized the man up, mid-fifties, neat, diminutive, meek. He obviously didn't like talking to the passengers, but he knew how to get them into his Qualis. Probably happy if he can hustle eight people, but will settle for six too. Raj Kumarji waited for the right moment, then haggled with the man for ₹25 each since he and his nephew didn't have big suitcases like the others. He had overheard the figure of ₹30 per ride, but was determined to pay less than the others who crowded into the van. Pyarelal was no fool. An extra fifty was an extra fifty, and the other passengers were waiting. He accepted the crumpled fifty-rupee note and held the door for the man and his tough-looking nephew.

On the way to Gurgaon, Raj Kumarji kept his eyes focused on the road ahead and plotted what he next had to do.

"This is a very very nice handset," Subinspector Shamsher Singh said, admiring Jan DeVries's titanium Vertu. "It is a beautiful, fine, black leather cover. Real alligator?"

Jan DeVries frowned. "What difference does that make?" he snarled.

"And now your other inside pocket, sir . . . A card key for the Radisson Gurgaon hotel? Ah, and another beautiful leather piece. Chaudhari, write this down: a black alligator wallet. And count the currency. Euros is it not? . . . Your wife? A lovely woman. Do you have children?"

"No children," Jan DeVries muttered, rubbing his wrists where the cuffs, just removed, had bound his hands.

"A pity. Children are a gift from God I think."

"Sir has two thousand euros in cash and fifteen hundred

rupees," constable Chaudhari interjected. "And several credit and bank cards whose numbers I have noted in the report."

"Excellent. Now your watch, please, sir," Singh said mildly, opening a large brown envelope, into which he dropped the phone, the card key and the wallet. "A beautiful, thin watch," he said, taking it from DeVries's hand. "Gold case. A Patek Philippe. I do not often get to hold one of these. What is Sir's business?"

"IT," DeVries said. "Software."

"Very interesting," Singh said. "Now the outside pockets of your beautiful jacket, sir."

"There's nothing in the pockets."

"Sir will hand over his jacket then, please."

"Do you have any idea what you are getting into?" DeVries asked, slipping out of the silk jacket and handing it across to Singh who immediately began to search its pockets. "False arrest, improper detainment, harassment. Hasn't anyone trained you about how to treat foreign nationals bringing business to your stone age country?"

"I thought you stated your pockets were empty," Singh said, holding up a fine linen kerchief and a folded sheet of paper.

"Am I supposed to declare a goddamn handkerchief and a piece of paper?"

"Sir was asked to empty his pockets. Chaudhari, what did Sir state?"

"Sir stated there was nothing left in his pockets," the constable said helpfully, reading from his form, a thin paper printed mostly in Hindi characters and now half-filled with miniscule writing from a ballpoint pen, none of it in English.

"An oversight I am sure," Singh said, tossing the kerchief and the folded paper into the brown envelope and reaching into the right hand pocket. He found a small plastic packet filled with suspicious white powder in it. He held it up and said, "And was this also an oversight? Constable, bag and tag this as evidence."

"So that's your game," DeVries growled. "Alright, enough is enough. When do I get my one phone call?"

"Sir has not been charged yet. First we will need to identify the white substance. Then we will decide if there are to be charges."

"How much?" Jan DeVries said. "Name your number."

Singh regarded him curiously. "You have been accused of soliciting illegal drugs—"

"Yes, by a truly reputable source—that reptile in the alley who probably—"

"—and you now deny knowledge of what you carry in your own pocket?"

"How much?" DeVries insisted. "The faster I get out of this hell-hole the better."

"Chaudhari, can you fetch us two masala tea?"

The constable got up from the table and left the men alone. Silence invaded the place and neither man spoke for a long time. Jan DeVries surveyed the dingy room, the wobbly table and the ugly walls which surrounded him. "How much?" he repeated.

Subinspector Singh had calculated how much the euros in the Dutchman's wallet were worth. About ₹120,000. He was in no hurry.

"Ah! Here is our chai," he said. "I have often found that

foreign guests prefer masala tea. Chaudhari, find some biscuits for us, please."

"I don't want any of your goddamn tea," Jan DeVries said. "Or your biscuits. I want to get out of this place right now. So tell me what is it going to take."

"Sir will please remove his belt and shoes."

Priyanka waited at Ricky Talsera's office door. She sat down on a sofa off to the left, closed her eyes, leaned her head on the backrest and had a little nap. A half hour passed, and then another fifteen minutes. The plink-plink-plink of stilettos on the marble foyer floor woke her up and she discovered the intimidating figure of The Destroyer towering over her. "Hi Shivani," she attempted drowsily.

"Where's Ricky?" Shivani snapped back, in no mood to exchange pleasantries. "He in there?"

"Yes," Priyanka said. "He asked me to wait. A long time ago. I'm still waiting for him to get off his call."

"Out of my way, Priyanka," Shivani said, and began knocking on the door impatiently. Inside the office, Ricky Talsera had no doubt about who was at the door. Steeling himself he opened it, only to find Priyanka and Shivani both standing there.

"Priyanka, I'm sorry," Ricky said. "I completely forgot."

"Okay, Priyanka," Shivani said. "Everybody's sorry, so beat it now. I've got important stuff to discuss with Ricky."

"But the dog?" Priyanka said. "You wanted to hear about Pushpa's dog."

"Priyanka, your dog will have to wait for the time being. Go back to your office and find somebody else to harass," Shivani said, before Ricky could get a word in. Priyanka looked at Ricky. He nodded.

"Let's get to it in the morning," he told her. "I'm sorry I made you wait. My mistake. I got distracted."

"No, no, Doctor," Priyanka said, and caught herself. "I mean Ricky. It's not a problem. I'll ping you tomorrow."

"Good idea," Shivani said, stepped inside and closed the door behind her. Without being invited, she took a seat across from Ricky at the blond wood desk. "I guess you want to know about RoodInfo?"

Ricky Talsera sat down. "Update me. Isn't your team supposed to be on top of this?"

"Monkey business!" Shivani exclaimed. "That little shit Vikram is back and he's trying to sabotage the project. He was seen in Jama Masjid with Jan DeVries a couple of hours ago. I have Jaitendra following Vikram, and Khaneja tailing DeVries. We think Vikram's responsible for the negative blogposts. I should know something later tonight."

"You're confident the status review will go well?"

"I'm cancelling it for the moment. Until we know how bad things are, my team is gonna hang back and do some bug-fixing instead."

"What are we going to tell DeVries?"

"Nothing for the moment. When he calls I'll meet up with him and distract him. Leave him to me."

Ricky's phone rang and he picked it up. "Yes," he said. "Of course I can speak to him, hold on a second." He placed his hand over the receiver of the phone. "Shiv, I need to take this. It's about building permits for the new campus. Please excuse me? Can we talk later when you know more?"

Shivani stood up. "Yes. I'll call you as soon as I hear anything useful." She stalked out of the office, closing Ricky's door loudly. Outside she dialled Nitin's number. "Get over to the small Newton conference room on the second floor in Building 3 right now. Don't make me wait," she told him.

14

That May of 1999, they rode up the valley called Joli La into an early thaw—where mud turned into stones the higher they climbed—and then marched through loose, punishing rocks as they pushed toward the *sangars* that stood along the ridge line. They never told you about the brilliant blue sky or the wild passage of clouds up there, or how the peaks stood out so clearly from so far away.

In the night, the Mirage 2000s came and pounded the enemy supply lines. You could hear the firepower from the passes below at sixteen thousand feet, bad guys getting hammered. Afterwards, you looked out onto the jagged peaks that bled crimson haze around their edges, framed by billowing grey cloud dispersed in the high atmosphere, then all went dark and black, quiet and starry again. Raw country, where the winds blew harsh and the cold dry air made your skin go leathery and your eyes burn. Headquarters said the enemy positions were full of army regulars, mujahideen, mercenaries and SSG operatives.

They had not told him how beautiful it would be in this

primitive place. It was a brutal terrain, but he found a rugged quality to it that a man could love; it was breathtaking and at the same time unforgiving. Some days he would watch a MiG-27 turn its wide balletic radius overhead, and he admired the delicate way they placed their bombs along the ridge. If you did not bomb the intruders into submission, then the infantry had to evict them. That was his job. But he loved the other beauty in the emptiness of the nights between skirmishes, when you had the time to follow the arcs of satellites overhead as they transited lazily among the constellations, girdled in stars, on a canvas vast like the universe.

When he slept, Jaitendra dreamt Boolean equations. He had learned them when he was quite young, in a Ramanujam club, and he used them in relation to nearly every decision he made in life. In the Army he chose his career options carefully, and as he took his promotions, he saw and did things he could not tell people back home—secret missions, midnight raids, interrogations of the really bad guys in dark rooms. He vowed that if he got through this incident in Kargil, he would quit and do the thing he truly loved, which was to fool around with computers. Preposterous, he knew, a Major prepared to trade in twelve years of exemplary service for the life of a tinkerer. He had only to stay long enough and one day he might be a General. He could have a fine white car with curtained windows and little flags on the front, and a Jonga full of uniformed soldiers, armed with sten guns, following him.

Experience had taught him that fighting a war could be broken down into little algorithms and heuristics, a network of binary decisions applied in split seconds. They had sent him to Kargil to retake the LoC. Often he sat silently, his INSAS rifle draped across his lap, and looked at the stars above and planned how he and his men would finish clearing the Tololing complex. "First bomb them into oblivion, break their will to fight, then overrun their positions." The way the headquarters put it to them, it sounded all too easy.

He would not speak of the dead he had seen as they moved up the *nullahs*, or of the lives he had ended. Let others do that. He had lost many good friends in the operations. Slowly they had retaken the ridges, under the barrage of artillery fire that crackled and boomed in the thin air. And when the last defenders had been pushed back, he wandered around the smoking, stinking ruins of their *sangars*. Among the rocks, he had seen corpses of people he knew, faces he had studied with in Germany years before, when they went as cadets to be trained by the Americans at a strange secret base in a forest called Hesse-Darmstadt. Dark violent skills, survival, hand-to-hand combat, weapons, psy-ops. Back then it was Indian guys versus Yankee guys, and they all hung together. He remembered Yousef, who played a phenomenal game of squash, unbeatable, now sprawled lifeless next to a crater. Mahmood, who knew by heart the works of Ghalib and Faiz, and given enough beer would declaim their verse in his eloquent voice from the head of the table, lay dead with a pistol in his hand, his legs blown away. There was bloody Sharif, who could have been a professional bowler if only he had quit the commandos and not stayed to defend this remote and devastated place, lying hollow-eyed next to an abandoned heavy machine gun. Among the last line of defenders, he found the remains of crudely dressed men he did not know, who carried antique rifles and wore the coarse cloth of mountain villages; fine snipers, men who would never go home, men whose corpses would decay unclaimed on these savage slopes.

He only wanted to be remembered as the man who brought all his boys home, but that was not to be true. Instead, they gave him a medal because he led one mad charge up a hill. And when he got home, time passed invisibly. He shook hands with the President, posed for endless photographs, endured backslapping and drinks sent to his table, called the grieving families of his lost men, went out on dates with naive girls who flashed their dark eyes at him and who seemed to fear him for what he had seen. Now that he was off active duty, he enrolled himself in an MBA course. But he never spoke about Kargil, and what he had seen there. Let others talk about it.

He settled back in Delhi and joined a sports club to stay in shape. It was there that he met Danny Khaneja. One day, after a judo class, Danny introduced him to Ricky Talsera, mentioned their startup, and Jaitendra joined the company—for no pay at first, since he knew very little about software—on the first day they were open for business. People would sometimes ask him about the famous charge, but he would ignore the question and would make them talk about code-writing. Eventually Kargil faded from people's conversations. But to his surprise, the software business turned out to be quite like the battleground, with similar binary decisions to make, just fewer bullets and bombs. The terrain was cut-throat, the adversaries were merciless and espionage played an occasional role.

One morning, during his fifth year at the company, Hari

Bhaiyya reported a break-in at Talsera. Some documents seemed to have been stolen. Khaneja somehow found out that a gang of Nigerians was responsible for it. He and Jaitendra paid the culprits' hideout a visit, retrieved the documents and returned thinking they had seen the end of it. But one night they walked into a bar after work, only to find the same guys sitting around. A confrontation ensued and though Jaitendra's close combat skills came in handy, Khaneja almost got killed in the melee.

It wasn't the first time Jaitendra's unique training had played a part in Talsera's survival. Over the years, he had dealt with everyone from lesser gangsters vying to take over the company's taxi contracts to corrupt customs inspectors, opportunistic lawyers and even some faked auto accidents. Sometimes a polite word was enough. Other times, the use of controlled force was the only answer.

Over the years he had become the most unusual kind of software architect. While he was always ready to be of help where troublemakers needed to be taken care of, he preferred the company of his programmers and engineers and, unless summoned, stayed cloistered with them, out of the mainstream of everyday business.

This time, following Khaneja's summons to stay with Shaitan Vikram, he hung behind unseen and waited patiently as Vikram madly keyboarded his user group posts at the internet café. The boy led him to a Dwarka apartment complex in Sector 6—DDA flats where a person could live anonymously and where neighbours didn't know each other. It was a grimy expanse of cookie-cutter crumbling blocks surrounded by weather-beaten trees and overgrown foliage. Perfect place to hide, Jaitendra thought, but now I've got you.

He shadowed Vikram to a courtyard surrounded by six identical buildings, observed him venture into an open staircase, climb five flights to the top floor, walk along an exposed outdoor passage, unlock a corner apartment door and go inside. Jaitendra moved to an adjacent building and found his way to the roof corner where he could see both sides of Vikram's apartment. Even though Vikram had closed off the balcony with dingy screens, Jaitendra could make out through the visible windows the faint glow of lights burning within. Not the same place where the driver Suresh said he lived; must be his workshop, Jaitendra thought. He texted Khaneja.

V has landed. Dwarka.

Khaneja replied immediately.

You'll stay with him?

Jaitendra smiled to himself and texted back.

Yes

Hari Bhaiyya made his rounds, starting at the roof of Building 3. It was empty; no problems there. He looked into the corner at the top of the enclosed staircase where his sleeping platform was located, next to the shelves where he kept his simple cooking implements; everything was as it should be. Down the steps to the fourth floor, through the broad room filled with empty cubicles—an hour earlier the place had been a beehive—across to the front staircase bathed in white light from the glass bricks, everything alright. Down one flight and he came upon his three goddesses. Their weekly meeting, usually a Wednesday or

Thursday after work, was in progress. They were seated around the round table in the tiny conference room at the front of the third floor, each with an identical yellow notebook open in front of her. He knew what they were doing. He nodded at them as he swept by, and continued on his round, floor by floor, checking that the big conference rooms were locked, seeing who was working late, checking in with the guards.

"Hari just went by," Harpreet said. "It must be 7:15."

"Adita, try and concentrate. We only have forty-five minutes until the taxi," Shoba said.

"I think we need to look more closely at the alternative energy sector," Adita said. "The potential for export business is enormous."

"So, what are our options?" Shoba said.

Adita turned the pages of her yellow notebook. She went on at length about the companies she had researched, then launched into a long explanation of how solar panels were installed. Finally Harpreet held up her hands in a "timeout" gesture.

"Adita, darling, you do realise we don't have all day, don't you?" Harpreet said. For a moment, their laughter filled the conference room.

Nitin sat at the dining-room table, at right angles to his father. They had shared a cup of tea in silence. A half-full plate of biscuits lay in front of them. The mantle clock ticked.

"This I do not understand," his father said. "Madamji called you in and asked you to resign? Without warning? You had no idea she would do this?"

"She is such a—" Nitin hesitated. "Bitchy woman," he said.

"Do not use that kind of language with me," his father said.

136

"But she *is* a bitch," Nitin insisted. "She didn't give me a choice. She told me she was tired of my behaviour and that I was holding back the group and that she had already given me many chances. I don't know what chances she was talking about. Then she made me sign a resignation letter."

"*Beta*, I do not understand what it is that you do or, for that matter, anything about your business. But this woman did not give any good reason for forcing you to leave your job."

"She told me we had a difference of styles," Nitin said.

"Son, I am not an educated man like you, but if it occurred as you say, I do not understand the logic of her decision."

"I do," Nitin said. "She hates me and does not want to work with me, no matter how dedicatedly and how well I work."

"Does she understand your situation, our circumstances?"

"I have no idea," Nitin said. "I can't figure this out. And now I don't know what to do. Any employer I apply to, will call Talsera and I will never get another job."

"What about that important project you were working on, the top-secret confidential one you were excited about but didn't want to discuss?"

Nitin reached for a biscuit. "I was so close to the answer," he said. "And yet, she fired me. Now I guess I'll never find out."

A woman wearing a yellow flight attendant's costume traversed the diagonal path in the courtyard below. Oversize shoulder bag, spike-heel shoes, hair drawn tight to form a neatly pinned bun at the back of her skull. Looked like someone just coming off from a shift. She glanced upward, her eyes sweeping the rooftop corner where Jaitendra casually leaned. At first he thought she had caught sight of him, but she did not look back up. Instead, she walked on, climbed the same stairs that Vikram had taken, reached the same level as his, walked down the open passage to the flat next to his, let herself in and disappeared inside.

Jaitendra waited on the roof for two more hours until his phone buzzed. A new SMS from Khaneja.

Another of those blogposts. It's time to shut him down.

Jaitendra stared across the divide at the passageway where the entry door to Vikram's lair lay. A faint ambient glow emanated from the apartment balcony. The tiny window that Jaitendra could see, was a soft amber rectangle in the dark wall.

TTYL, he texted Khaneja, and powered off the mobile.

As he prepared to leave the rooftop, the door to Shaitan Vikram's apartment opened and his angular, unmistakable figure emerged. It slammed the door, locked it shut and then stole away to the staircase. Jaitendra watched him walk out to the main road.

Quick binary decision: the kid or the apartment?

Winner: the apartment.

Jaitendra made his way down the staircase, walked behind Vikram's building, took the centre stairs Vikram wouldn't be using, and stood in front of his door in no time. He felt in his left-hand pocket for the familiar set of lockpicks he always kept with himself. But before he could take them out, the door to the adjoining apartment opened about six inches and a woman peered out at him. She had changed from her yellow outfit and now wore blue jeans and a tight black T-shirt. Her braided hair hung delicately over her left shoulder. She looked quite attractive.

"You're not a cop," she said. Jaitendra didn't reply. "You're more like those guys who protect important people, no? I bet you're a private eye. I saw you up on the roof when I came home and then I saw you sneak around the back of the building."

"You're not a flight attendant," Jaitendra said. "And you're pretty damn observant."

"He won't be back for at least an hour, maybe more. You want to come in and wait?"

"What if I'm a serial killer?"

"I'm a pretty good judge of character," she said. "I meet a lot of people in my work. You look okay to me. Come in. I might have some useful information for you."

"Alright," Jaitendra said. "Five minutes."

"Hooda," the voice said.

"Mr Hooda, it's Dilbar Khaneja. How are you, sir?"

"Danny," Ajit Hooda said warmly. "Very well, what a pleasure to hear from you. How is your father? Still going to all the matches?"

"Great, great. And, yes, mostly with the grandchildren. He goes to a few one-days, but hates the T20s." Danny smiled to himself.

"He was always the best," Ajit Hooda said. "His late cut was so elegant and he could place the ball just where he wanted. I am sure you didn't call me to talk about cricket, though. How can I be of service?"

"I have a foreign client in a bit of a situation over at the Jama Masjid police *thana*."

"And you need my help."

"I need you to make sure he stays there a little while longer until I sort out some business connected to him. Then let me know how to take this guy off your hands. He's prepared to cooperate."

"I'll have my PA make some inquiries," Hooda said. "Call me back in an hour. I'm sure we can work it out. And send my regards to your dad. Tell him Hooda remembers."

"I will, sir, and all the best to Mrs Hooda."

How odd, Jaitendra thought, looking around the apartment. You could never tell what went on behind closed doors. It was hardly what he expected from a place in a dusty Dwarka block. The walls were white and bare; freshly painted; no stains or holes; decorated by two framed prints which said "Louvre Paris" across the bottom in modern letters, by artists he didn't recognise; one poster looked like a pond with lilies painted with colourful smudges; the other a window with a table and a bowl of fruits; both could have been drawn by a kid for all he knew. The floor had been sanded and stained with dark finish, and under the modern couch on which he was seated, a simple but tasteful Rajasthani carpet with green chevron design rested.

It appeared she read a lot. A wide bookshelf stood against the wall, filled with volumes of different sizes. On the stylish teak coffee-table before him, next to the teapot and teacup that she had placed there just a few moments ago, he saw a copy of something by an author named Proust. Jaitendra picked it up and hefted it—a fat book with many pages and tiny print. "This any good?" he asked and she shook her head. "No television?" he asked, putting the book down.

She pointed at a closed, wood cabinet. "I like to keep it hidden," she said.

"No computer?" he asked.

"In my bedroom," she said.

"How'd you get a place like this?" Through the doorway he could see that the kitchen was in excellent repair: new, stainless-steel appliances; blue-tiled countertops; nice, white china on the shelves; glass jars of lentils, rice, beans, pickle and masala packets his Mom used to have arranged inside small cabinets. A familiar smell drifted out into the living room. She had something simmering, maybe a dal.

"The furniture came from a diplomat who was going home and didn't want to ship it back. I bought it all from him. A gay boy I met, who decorates sets for Bollywood flicks, helped me remodel. He had some guys come in during the day, so we didn't attract any attention. You done asking questions?" Jaitendra nodded, but he wondered about her. She was hiding something.

Her name was Neha. She was twenty-nine years old; from Meerut. She had come to Delhi to enroll herself in an academy which trained people to work in the airline industry when she was nineteen. She'd quickly discovered they wanted subservient girls and not those with opinions, or who, like her, spoke their mind. Yet she completed the course and learned to wear her hair and uniform the way they wanted, learned to greet people, to make safety announcements over the PA system, to serve drinks gracefully, to roll carts down the aisle and collect people's rubbish, learned how to help the pregnant and the handicapped, and what to do in case of over-the-water landings.

But she hated the pompous types who interviewed her. She had no trouble reading the lascivious looks of men who did not hesitate to hint that all it would take was a fast transaction on an office couch and she could be sure of a position immediately. She never met the right person doing the hiring, and so she never got a job.

One afternoon, she happened to be sipping coffee next to an attractively dressed woman in a Café Coffee Day outlet and they struck up a conversation. Neha did not withhold her opinion of the people she was meeting. The well-dressed woman clucked sympathetically and agreed that it's not as glamorous working as an air-hostess as people think. She herself had considered it, but was much happier working simply as a hostess. Before leaving, she gave Neha the business card of a lady who worked at an export company and who sometimes needed smart girls to help the firm's out-of-town visitors who somehow seemed to like meeting flight attendants. Eventually, she built her own business by word-of-mouth, and soon had a good reputation.

Neha never told her family about her job; she simply pretended to be working in an airline. She bought a yellow outfit from a Jet Airways girl and a red one from a Kingfisher girl, and she often showed up for her dates in a uniform, as if she had just got off from work. They seemed to like that fantasy. She found she could make as much money in a day like this as she would have made in a month as an air hostess, and that too, without having to serve packaged meals to impolite people. In fact, now she was the one being served expensive meals at the coolest restaurants and people were nice to her. She also always had money, and was able to save enough even after sending some home. Whenever she made the three-hour trip back home to Meerut, she took along sweets and bangles, wore a sari, played with her nieces and nephews, and made excuses about why she never married. "I'm always flying away somewhere," she told them. "Nobody would ever marry me!"

Jaitendra again confronted another one of those binary decisions: should he stay or should he go?

Stay.

"Yeah, I think I'm done asking questions," he said and took a sip of the tea. "Now tell me what you know about the boy next door."

It would not be long now, Jan DeVries thought, staring at the pitiful chamber in the *thana* where he had been sequestered. Somebody would notice soon enough. His driver, Shivani, Khaneja, those idiots at Talsera, somebody! Perhaps it might be even Berthe in Rotterdam, trying to figure out why he had not made his daily call. She may, by now, have even phoned his office in a panic and was probably hitting the martinis earlier than usual. Anyway, eventually somebody was bound to come and get him out of this shithole, and then he would do some damage in return. First, he would call the ambassador and order this man Singh's head on a platter. He would call the news media and give them a story of false imprisonment, fraud and extortion that would be all over the international airwaves. He would ruin careers. He would make people think twice about doing business in this third-rate country. He had understood what the police officer was trying to do—first intimidate him by taking his belt and shoes and then hold him until he begged to be set free. But he would not give in so easily. Time was his friend; the longer they were going to hold him, the more trouble they would be in. He understood they were waiting for him to surrender, but he would offer them no satisfaction. Let them try their infantile tactics. He was not some over-privileged college student caught in a compromising position. Jan DeVries would not be manipulated.

A cockroach scurried over his foot and he gave a startled yelp as he jumped, and fell back into his chair, banging his knees painfully against the underside of the sticky wood table in the process. He stood up and his casual trousers slipped over his hips and he frantically grabbed them, bunching them up at the front before they could get down to his knees. He was hungry and thirsty and the walls stank. The air was stale in the windowless room. But Jan DeVries would not give in.

Out in the parking, the red-turbaned Sikh awoke with a start and consulted his watch. The client had been gone for more than two hours already. He called his mobile number.

Inside the police *thana*, the constable yet again heard a buzzing sound from the brown envelope containing Jan DeVries's possessions. It wasn't the first time the phone had gone off and the noise irritated him. He fished into the envelope, found the power switch on the expensive device and turned it off.

The Sikh called the Radisson deskman and reported that DeVriesji hadn't come back from Karim's. The deskman called Danny Khaneja.

"Your driver can come back in," Khaneja told the deskman. "I'll make sure the guest gets a ride home."

Raj Kumarji studied the signboard which showed the map of the sector, and eventually found the block he wanted. He could not tell the distance precisely, but he was confident a cycle-rickshaw driver would know the way. Off to his side Mahesh smoked a cigarette, waiting for orders. Fixing his calculating gaze on the unfinished concrete skeletons which towered overhead, Raj Kumarji wondered which one of them was his destination. While he understood the need for progress, he could not fathom why people would choose to live under such chaotic conditions. It was all noise and mud and people moving too quickly. Too many cars, too many two-wheelers, too many traditions forgotten. He looked at his nephew in the Megadeth T-shirt. Who would hire a boy like him? Who would marry their daughter to him?

"I've seen the guy next door quite a few times, sneaking around," Neha began.

"His name's Vikram."

"He never introduced himself, that was strange. Guys usually want to meet me, or at least they smile. This Vikram fellow doesn't seem the slightest bit interested. He sees me, he fumbles with his keys and hurries inside. I don't know if he sleeps there, but I see him leaving some mornings. The first month he was here, he kept getting deliveries, boxes and boxes. Bumped around in there for a few days. Then he closed off the balcony. Any of this help?"

"None of it," Jaitendra said. "What else do you have for me? Your five minutes are almost up."

"What makes you think I'm not an air hostess?"

"Your shoes were all wrong, and the bag, and the uniform. Flight attendants wear closed-toe shoes, not spiky heels. They have wheely bags, not shoulder bags like working girls'. And your uniform is out of date, not that your clients are ever going to say anything."

"Maybe it's my other job."

"Right," Jaitendra said, rising. "I'm leaving."

"Wait," she said. "I can help you."

"I don't need any help."

"He's not going to get back for at least an hour."

"And you know this because?"

"Because he pretty much lives on the tandoori rotis he gets from the *dhaba* down the road. I've watched him for six months, his behaviour hasn't changed. He also has paan after dinner. He stays away at least an hour. I'll make a deal with you. I stand guard, look out for you. If he gets back early I'll warn you. But I'd want to see inside his place. I want to see what you find."

"Why are you so curious?"

"I'm a student of human nature. Okay? Take it or leave it."

Jaitendra smiled at her. A binary decision. She had intelligent eyes, and she didn't seem to be intimidated. "*Theek hai*," he said. "You stand guard and I'll let you look around inside after I'm done."

To his surprise, she leaned across the couch, put her hand gently on the back of his neck and kissed him firmly on the lips. Then she sat back.

"Nice to meet you, partner. I will be back in a flash."

She got up and went into her room and was back in five minutes. She had changed into the yellow Jet Airways uniform and now had a rolling bag with her. Jaitendra noticed she had also slipped on a pair of closed-toe shoes.

"One question," she said after she had pulled him out onto the balcony. She pointed down towards one corner of the courtyard. "You see that black man standing in the shadows over there?"

"Of course I do," Jaitendra said. "He's a Nigerian. Been shadowing me on and off for years."

"Are you going to finish him off?"

"No. Not yet, at least. I'm going to keep leading him around until I figure out what to do with him."

"So I just pretend he's not there."

"Correct," Jaitendra said.

The RayBan sunglasses, the wallet, the opulent mobile phone, the hotel key, the linen handkerchief, the belt, the shoes, the white powder in the clear plastic evidence bag, the folded piece of paper. Subinspector Singh looked at the contents of the brown envelope laid out on his desk. Had he miscommunicated with the *firangi*? He had given the man every opportunity, but he had remained obstinate. It could have been so simple, but the man would not budge. The constable had confirmed the man was registered at the Radisson Gurgaon, though strangely, the Foreigner Regional Registration Office had reported that he changed his hotel just one night after his arrival. Very suspicious, Subinspector Singh thought. Smuggling? Illegal diamonds? Drug trafficking? The man was from the Netherlands, where marijuana and hashish were freely traded, where addicts were given free heroin, where people could legally commit suicide under the supervision of a physician. A bizarre little country with mysterious laws.

Absently, Subinspector Singh unfolded the paper and examined what was written there. Three sentences scrawled in a schoolboy hand. He could not understand the language, something about invoicing and error codes, password-protected formulae, upcharges and back valuation. But he could see one word which stood out: RoodInfo. He opened his personal laptop, which he had handpicked from the evidence room some months earlier and had caused to 'go lost,' and googled the name. Instantly a site from a company jumped forward and he clicked through it, not totally clear what it was all about. At the lower right he read the words *Powered by Talsera*, and he googled 'Talsera.' It seemed he had trapped the man in the midst of an act of corporate espionage. He congratulated himself on his brilliant luck. Now Subinspector Singh had something he could leverage.

He walked out of his office happily, passing the area where the constables stood around discussing the latest cricket scores. "Hold all my calls," he told them and opened the door to the tiny room where Jan DeVries sat. The room was hot and the air inside thick with the smell of the Dutchman's sweat and his European cologne and the memories of thousand other interrogations.

DeVries raised his eyes and Subinspector Singh knew the man had not softened. "I hope you've come to your senses and are letting me out of this rubbish heap."

"I cannot be helping sir without his cooperation," Singh replied. "There is nothing more you want to tell me about your visit to Old Delhi? Why you came all the way from Gurgaon when your business is down there? Who you met or the purpose of your visit?"

"Tourism. I like spicy food."

"I believe sir is withholding evidence. I believe that sir—" Singh was interrupted by the caller tune of his mobile phone. He looked down at the screen. "Sir will excuse me," he said and left the room.

"You can believe what you goddamn well want to," Jan DeVries growled to the empty room. "You're not getting anything from me."

Outside the room the Subinspector answered his call. "Yes, sir?" he asked solicitously.

"You're holding a *firangi*," the caller said. "Someone whose welfare I am interested in. You follow?"

"Of course, sir."

"You will hold him in isolation until you hear from me later tonight. Then you will release him. Do you understand? You do not harm him, but you do not set him free until I say so. Are we clear?"

"Yes, sir."

"Very good," said Ajit Hooda and the line went dead.

16

It took Jaitendra all of thirty-four seconds to pick the top lock, and another twenty-eight to open the bottom lock. Once he was in, he secured the door behind him.

An eerie, blue-green light hung in the room, casting gloomy shadows in every corner. The room temperature was cool, though not cold. He had left the computers on, expecting to be back soon, never dreaming that someone would raid his secret command post while he was gone. Cheap folding tables, full of weird blinking boxes connected by clusters of cables and strewn with papers, lined two walls. Fat extension cords and multi-plug power strips criss-crossed the floor. Fans whooshing above filled the room with a uniform, ambient sound, which was punctuated only by the occasional plink of a device resetting itself. Little red-and-green lights seemed to dance everywhere. An open tool box, with rolls of black electrical tape and pliers and screwdrivers and colourful plastic pieces, lay on the floor below a table. On one of the walls, two large whiteboards had been mounted, filled with a myriad of scribblings and jottings that only their author could decipher. Across the room, a single easy chair had been placed next to a wobbly Chinese halogen floor lamp. Strewn about the chair were dozens of discarded glossy computer magazines. In the unfurnished corner sat a pile of trash—a pyramid of Domino's Pizza boxes around which the faint stench of rancid tomato sauce lingered.

Three large monitors, set side by side, framed the corner where the tables met; a leather rolling office-chair stood in front of them. A ridiculous Logitech wireless keyboard undulated in front of the centre screen. The left screen displayed some online role-playing game in progress—a parallel world of passageways and demons lurking behind Neolithic pillars, of galaxies and occasional blasts, light years off, visible through open porticos. A state-of-the-art Bose headset, connected by a hot yellow cord, had been tossed onto a stack of manuals, and a shiny new joystick occupied the position to the left of the keyboard. On the right, a well-worn tracking-ball mouse lurked, its orb glowing a shimmering opal.

The centre monitor displayed five windows. On the top-right corner, a South Korean lady in a porn chat asked for money to buy a business-class ticket to visit him; she included her bank account number for his convenience. A teenage girl in Sao Paolo suggested he might enjoy looking more closely at a film of her bikini waxing, in the top-left corner. In the bottom-left window, an obese Romanian woman danced naked in front of a webcam, her overwhelming breasts jiggling in close-up. In the bottom-right corner, a casino game was in progress—Blackjack—with some sort of an automated program running and a robot racking up virtual winnings into hundreds of millions. And occupying the centre of the screen was the site where the negative blogposts by KnightTuring had been written. He was obviously following the comments.

Jaitendra immediately recognised the contents of the right-hand screen: the RoodInfo code displayed in the left half and in the right, Talsera's internal emails constantly updated. Off to the right of the screens, a new HP colour printer sat atop its packing box, primed and fully loaded, ready to churn out documents. In the paper tray he found a printout of a Nordic girl sunbathing topless. He shook his head in wonder: if only Vikram had used his prodigious talents to do good in the world.

Quickly, Jaitendra moved to the tiny bedroom which contained a single steel-framed folding bed with rumpled bed sheets on it, and a folding chair piled with soiled clothing. A lone pair of sandals sat at the foot of the bed, next to another ugly Chinese floor lamp. The rest of the room acted as a dumping ground for the packing materials of everything that came into the flat. Big cardboard boxes, Styrofoam pieces, plastic bags, crumpled papers, rough plastic cords, glossy printed product cartons and empty CD and DVD packages littered everywhere in the room. Detritus of consumer culture. Jaitendra peered into the bathroom. It seemed it had never been cleaned. Outside the door stood irregular stacks of industrial toilet paper rolls and bundles of cheap paper towels carrying the logo of a Bengali restaurant supply company. In the tiny kitchen he found a tall black plastic bag stuffed with fetid trash. The sink was full of unwashed glasses and crusty tableware which Vikram had probably stolen from restaurants. He lifted a dingy towel with his pen point, set it down gingerly. There was a box of empty Thums Up bottles next to the refrigerator, inside which Jaitendra found half-eaten sweets and covered containers of dead take-away food. In the freezer he saw three flavours of ice cream. A tea pot on the counter was still warm.

Beside the doorway to the balcony, he discovered a brand new generator next to a freestanding air-conditioning unit and a large industrial battery array, all connected by cabling to something outside. Jaitendra opened the door to find an elaborate system of solar panelling occupying nearly every inch of space, but blocked from view by flimsy screens. It was ingenious, he thought, how Vikram had set everything up such that he could move the sliding panels and adjust the components to harness the sunlight, so that he wasn't relying solely on the power supply or the noisy generator.

Jaitendra came back to the main room and sat down in Vikram's chair. He stared thoughtfully at his surroundings, swinging slowly from left and right. What had he missed? What had he forgotten? He went back to his training days and recalled how to search a room, the elementary things. He looked under the tables and started shifting around things. Below the keyboard he found a bulky envelope fastened with thick tape. It contained $18,000 in American hundred dollar bills. Jaitendra stuffed the envelope into his coat pocket. Now what? More searching or defensive action? Another binary decision. Defensive action.

Jaitendra spent the next fifteen minutes changing all the passwords on the open computers. For such a complex arrangement, it proved to be simpler than he had thought. All the programs were fortuitously logged into with admin privileges. Once the passwords were reset, Jaitendra took out a 40 GB flash drive he had brought along, popped it into a USB port and began to copy the files he wanted to examine later. While the files were downloading, he snapped photos of everything in the flat using his phone's camera. He sent the photos to Danny Khaneja. Not a half minute later, Khaneja texted him back.

Bring him in to the office. Einstein conf room, building 3, 9pm.

Jaitendra turned back to the centre screen and began to methodically delete the negative blogposts. Just as he was finishing, a frantic rapping came from the door.

"He's back!" Neha said from the balcony. "He just went into the stairwell. You have about a minute!" Jaitendra heard her walk to her own apartment door, open it and go inside. He waited.

Subinspector Shamsher Singh marveled. He knew he had not told Ajit Hooda about the *firangi* he had captured. He knew Hooda had spies everywhere, but he did not know how the boss of Old Delhi had found out so quickly. It was a miracle, an astounding display of the man's power and reach. Another reason to be extremely careful. Hooda knew everything; Hooda could not be deceived. The phone call had been a kind of warning to him, an unspoken threat, a demonstration of just how little enterprise on his own part would be tolerated. He called the constable outside his office and told him to bring Lateef. Minutes later Lateef, cowering, was shown into the office, a large purple lump forming on his forehead where he had been struck during his 'arrest.' Lateef knew enough to keep his mouth shut until spoken to.

"You are free to go," Singh said. "You are no longer needed on this case." He picked up the sealed evidence bag and removed the plastic envelope of white powder which Lateef had planted in Jan DeVries's pocket. "I believe this belongs to you?"

Lateef eyed the subinspector warily. "No," he said. "It is not mine!"

Singh placed the envelope on the far edge of his desk and turned away to face the window. "I do not know what it is, or to whom it belongs," he said, looking out. "It is of no further use to me. It is to me as if it did not ever exist." When he turned back, the envelope had disappeared. "Now get out of here." And Lateef disappeared.

But he was back within twenty minutes.

"A man asked me to give you this letter," he said, passing over a page, which the subinspector took.

"When?"

"Just now, after I left the *thana*," Lateef said. "A well-dressed Indian man who spoke excellent Hindi. An educated man wearing expensive western clothing."

"Tell me exactly what he said."

Lateef squinted his eyes, and tried to recollect. He had taken a sniff of the white powder as soon as he had found a hidden doorway. He was not quite sure what he had heard. Everything was so bright and brilliant. "Said?"

"His words, you fool! What exactly did he tell you?"

"I think he said, '*Oye*, take this letter to the policeman,' and gave me twenty rupees."

"That is all he said? Nothing more?"

Lateef searched his memory. "He also said, 'Do not hand it to anyone else. Only the policeman who struck you outside Karim's. I will be watching you.'"

"Describe the man."

"He looked like all rich men do to me. Like a movie star. Young and handsome and very sure of himself."

Subinspector Singh opened the note and read it.

Sir, I may be of some help to you regarding the prisoner named DeVries. I will come to the thana at 18:30 to meet you. Sincerely, Dilbar Khaneja

Khaneja? Where had he heard that name before?

"You're not going to like this," Rajan Abraham said, seated across from Ricky Talsera. He had shown up unannounced at Ricky's office, an unprecedented event. While the two men had started the company together, with the silent participation of Danny Khaneja, and though they were immensely fond of each other, their areas of responsibility were so distant that they rarely had occasion to meet face to face. They usually met only in larger meetings. It was their wives who ensured they kept in touch.

"Got to be about the RoodInfo job," Ricky said.

"How'd you guess that?" Rajan asked.

"What else could it be? It's a mess," Ricky said.

Abraham bobbed his leg, looked everywhere but at his partner and said, "You remember I had a kid, thought he could track down who was breaking into our email and putting internal stuff on the net?"

"Of course I do. How's that going?"

"That's the problem. The boy was very close to the answer. Pretty inventive, really. He'd set some traps, put out some bait and was closing in. Kind of like a bloodhound. We almost had the intruder."

"Almost," Ricky said. "That's not good enough."

"I think he needed another half a day, just a few hours, and he would have figured it all out. Just a little more time."

"So what's the problem? Give it to him. The status review's been put off. Khaneja's close to nailing Vikram. Jaitendra's somewhere, doing something, don't ask me what. DeVries is bound to reappear sooner or later. Let the kid carry on."

"But Shivani fired him this afternoon."

"Wait a minute! She can't do that. Wasn't HR involved? Nobody else consulted?"

"Don't ask me, Ricky. If I could understand her . . ."

"You're telling me she terminated the boy without telling HR, you or me?"

Rajan Abraham nodded a yes. "She even had him sign a resignation letter."

"How'd the kid take it?"

"Cleaned out his things fast and left without a word to anybody. Isn't picking up his cell. Nobody else can take up where he left off. I had him doing this all by himself. I was thinking of sending Hari Bhaiyya over to his house."

"To say what? Oops, we're sorry, you're reinstated? No, Hari won't be able to pull it off. One of us will have to go. And then, we also have The Destroyer to contend with. Did you talk to Khaneja about this?"

"Ricky, this only happened a couple of hours ago. I just found out from one of the other boys."

"We need that blogger's name. Whoever it is has the power to kill the RoodInfo account and damage our reputation. Bring the boy back on as an independent contractor."

Rajan Abraham considered the suggestion. "There's still Shivani," he said. "She'll raise a stink because we're going against her decision. I hadn't told anybody that Nitin was working on this. It was kind of hush-hush."

"Wait. Nitin? That boy who idolises Hitler, the one who always follows me around at company parties, trying to talk to me? He's the one you were using?"

"Ricky, the kid's barely twenty-six. You think he knows what he's saying or doing? Trust me, he is quite good. He has the aptitude and loves technology. We need people like him."

"Except that he's a sociopath."

"Oh, we can mentor him. But anyway, we need him now to catch the blogger. The Dutch guy is an asshole. If we don't stop the posts, he'll put all kinds of pressure on us and not pay us for the work already done. Or he may even pull the plug on us completely."

"Let's keep trying Nitin's mobile, then. I'll think of something to say to Shivani in the meanwhile. The guys making any progress on the release?"

"We were ready for the status review today—we always are—but we can always use more time."

"Okay. Let's have a beer when all this is over."

"If it ever is all over, and we're still standing," Rajan Abraham said.

Ricky nodded, said a quick goodbye and sat alone in his office. He knew that RoodInfo was short of cash and was looking for a way to not pay. He worried that if the account disappeared, he would have forty idle engineers on his hands. Besides, he would have the personal pain of losing a large account. Life at the top, he thought.

Karim's again, but this time Khaneja sat by himself, lost in thought, picking at a plate of kebab. He suspected a deeper involvement between Shivani and DeVries, but he was not so sure whether or not she had any knowledge of Vikram's treachery. The only way to be certain was to put the players together in one place and watch them. Then he would know. He would need to get DeVries out of the police *thana* and down to Gurgaon for that to happen. But he had an hour to sit and think, to fit the pieces together. And he could not wait to get his hands on Shaitan Vikram.

His mobile rang and he picked it up immediately. It was Hari Bhaiyya. "Sir, Shivani madam has fired an engineer without permission."

"Who?" Khaneja asked. "When?"

"Someone who was helping to find the mischief-maker. Today. She didn't ask anyone."

"Hari, I want you to have the Einstein conference room ready for me at 8 p.m. Make sure two or three of your best guards stay on duty late. We're having guests and I may need them. Is Ricky Sir still in his office?"

"Yes," Hari Bhaiyya said. "Do you need me to tell him anything?"

"No, thanks"

Khaneja called Ricky Talsera. "Shivani's colluding with DeVries and DeVries with Vikram. I can prove it. We need to have a meeting with everybody tonight to put the pieces together.

160

Trust me, some smiles are going to be shattered. Can you have Shivani in Einstein at eight?" he asked.

A mischevous look swept across Ricky's face. "Will be my pleasure," he said.

17

After she left Ricky, Shivani sat in her own office twiddling her thumbs for five minutes until she got fed up. What difference did it make whether she was here or there? In her search for Jan DeVries, she'd been out to Old Delhi sweating like a pig all afternoon, and now Danny Khaneja had her standing by, waiting for nothing. So she left Building 3, found her driver and had him take her home, which wasn't far away. She took a long shower and tried not to think about what she was going to say to DeVries the next time they met. This whole RoodInfo account was flying out of control. Besides, Vikram's return had introduced particularly unsavory complications.

The idea of Jaitendra skulking around offended her. He had a sinister past and was a dangerous, circumspect and unpredictable commodity. He also had the ear of Ricky Talsera. Shivani didn't trust him and knew she had better keep an eye on him as well. She toweled off, admiring her naked body in the full-length mirror of her dressing room. She had become more comfortable sunbathing on the beaches of Deauville than on the sands of Goa, and she wondered whether to take another holiday at that sweet little hotel she had stayed in at in Cap d'Antibes. It had a view of the promenade and the yacht harbour, and a little café downstairs which she liked and where she could sit at a table all afternoon in the shade of an old tree and drink pastis as men walked by and made eyes at her. Europeans were so much more direct. What about Jan DeVries? As long as he was not sabotaging her project, she might take up with him as he had so frequently suggested. He wanted them to meet in the Seychelles, do some snorkeling, stay at a five-star resort. She might give him a chance. Shivani chose some lacy black underwear and opened her closet looking for something cute and sexy. Then her mobile buzzed, a new SMS.

RoodInfo mtg 8pm be on time pls, Einstein. Ricky

Okay, Shivani thought, time to rethink my outfit.

"Nalini darling!"

"Shaalu! I was going to call you!"

"Have you got five minutes? There's some stuff I need to ask you."

"Yes, sure. I have something to ask you too."

"Do you have any idea why Ricky just left me a message to say he will work late tonight?" Shaalu asked.

"I can guess," Nalini Abraham said. "That RoodInfo client. It's got the whole office on edge. Has he told you much about it?"

"What he hasn't told me I've seen on the internet. Somebody's been trashing Talsera anonymously on some blog."

"I saw that too. It's Shivani's job, right?"

"Yes, unfortunately. I don't know why they keep her around," Shaalu said.

"She was in at the beginning, one of the first hires. You know how loyal those guys are."

"But how many jobs has she brought in lately?"

"And what does she do to get them?" Both women giggled.

"She's certainly rich enough. You know she inherited quite a fortune from her parents. She doesn't need the job."

"I don't think she would be missed," Nalini said. "I wouldn't miss her. Rajan wouldn't. He hides in his office when he hears she's around. You know Hari Bhaiyya has a standing order to keep Rajan posted on her whereabouts so he can avoid her."

"Today she may have gone too far," Shaalu said.

"What? She had sex with one of the peons? That was mean of me. I didn't say that."

"Not as bad. Ricky told me she terminated somebody on her own today."

"Sounds like Shivani. Taking matters into her own hands."

"We can only hope for the worst."

"What else did you want to ask me?"

"Jodhpur Tool and Die. I bought it at thirty-eight. It hit seventy-one yesterday. Sell?" Shaalu asked.

"Not yet," Nalini said. "Wait for one hundred. It'll get there. Be patient."

"What was it that *you* wanted to ask me?"

"Did you get the invitation for Harpreet's wedding?"

"Oh my God, I did. All those red and gold sparkles. Really really glittery."

"You saw his parents left her last name off it?"

"I saw that. I guess they want to pretend she's not Hindu. Are you guys going?"

"I don't think so. We'll send a nice gift."

"We were thinking the same thing. But somebody from top management should go," Shaalu said.

"What about the Khanejas?"

"I'll ask them. They get along with everybody."

"What a shame we can't make Shivani go."

"Yes, and tell her she has to wear a sari."

"She'd probably pick one up at Chanel."

"Oh, by the way, I must show you this new ring Rajan bought for me—Brazilian brown diamonds in a titanium band. It's exquisite."

"Promise me you'll wear it when we see you for Diwali."

"Sure. Oh! I hear the kids. Have to run! Let me call you later. Byeee!"

Raj Kumarji was puzzled when the rickshaw driver dropped him on the street he had asked for. There were three buildings with the name 'Talsera' on them. A patient man by nature, he walked to the same chai wallah where Ricky and Jaitendra liked to go, sat down on a red plastic stool and sent his nephew to get two cups of masala chai. As he waited, he observed. It soon became clear that many young people were filing out of Building 3, which also had the business name in large, mirrored letters, running in a vertical strip along the modern façade. He had not expected the company to have three buildings in the same sector. He did not know that Talsera had offices in four European cities and four in America as well.

He noticed that Building 3 had a guardhouse at the entrance. After he had finished his cup of chai, he snapped his fingers, handed Mahesh a piece of paper and said, "Dial the number written here and give the phone to me when it starts ringing. Then go over there and talk to the guard and see if you can find out where the office of the owner of this company is located."

As Raj Kumarji proceeded with his call, speaking secretively into the phone, Mahesh meandered over to the guard house and tried to start up a conversation with Security Guard #8 Raheem. "Well?" asked Raj Kumarji, when the young man returned.

"He told me to go away," said Mahesh. Raj Kumarji nodded, his low expectation of the youth's potential unaltered. "He told me to stop asking questions; threatened he would call the police."

Raj Kumarji handed back the mobile phone. "Now we wait," he said. "Watch for my signal. If we encounter any resistance, any at all, be prepared to grab Adita and let nobody else get near her. She will leave this place with us, and only us."

Mahesh nodded; he knew enough not to ask for more information. He could read the tense twitches at the corners of the old man's mouth. If he knew one thing about his uncle, it was that those twitches meant trouble was on its way.

Some time later, an official-looking white Ambassador, with two uniformed constables in the front, pulled up across from Building 3. A ghostly silhouette could be seen through the sheer curtains that covered the rear windows of the vehicle.

The occupant of the back seat was ASI Ramesh Thakur, who had earlier been warned by the Brigadier that a call from Raj Kumarji might be forthcoming. The call had come while Thakur was engaged in a challenging, athletic tantric position with his girlfriend, as part of the regular afternoon liaison he believed his wife was unaware of, which was not the case. Much to his girlfriend's disappointment, the ASI had leapt out of bed and taken the call. Thakur owed the Brigadier big time, a debt resulting from a particularly sticky incident involving hijacked Chinese truck parts. The Brigadier had made the whole mess go away—no arrest, no trial, no jail, no black spot on his record. Henceforth, if the Brigadier called, ASI Thakur was his man.

He had brought along two young and ambitious constables who followed orders and did not ask questions. On the phone, it had sounded like a simple enough situation: an old dude from Rajasthan needed to take his daughter back home. She had fallen victim to a fast-living city boy. Thakur suspected that the girl was probably on drugs all the time, went to nightclubs, had casual sex, and wore short skirts.

ASI Thakur remained inside the car and occupied himself with texting his girlfriend. The constables got out and looked around, up and down the street, across to the chai wallah, and the older of the two nodded at Raj Kumarji. Motioning to his nephew to follow, Raj Kumarji walked in a proud manner—back straight, eyes fixed forward, almost a military march—across the muddy road, through the concrete gateway, up to the window of the small blockhouse where Security Guard #8 Raheem sat. The police constables followed him, but held back at a respectful distance.

"I demand to see the owner of this company," Raj Kumarji said. "Now. And if you do not tell him I am here, I will have those cops order you to do so."

Security Guard #13 Vartan, who stood outside the blockhouse and exchanged curious glances with his colleague. This looked complicated.

"Hurry up!" Raj Kumarji said. "I do not have all day." A group of laughing employees filed by him, their daily work done, but they went silent as they looked curiously at the visitors, sensed the tension in the air, hurried away and did not look back. Raj Kumarji stood at attention, waiting. He eyed both the security guards, who had no desire to defy the old fellow in the turban and grey jacket who had an undeniable air of authority about him. The young man in the Megadeth T-shirt who hovered behind him and the two constables loitering over by the gate added a note of menace to the situation.

"Please wait," Security Guard #8 Raheem said as he dialled Hari Bhaiyya's number. Soon the problem would become Hari's.

Shaitan Vikram shifted the bag of bananas from his right arm to his left and fumbled with his keys. He had some trouble getting the top lock open, but finally it clicked. Then one-handedly he found the key for the bottom lock and worked on it, juggling the bag of bananas. This one always stuck and it took a special twist at the end, with just the right amount of pressure, to open it. He looked left and right down the passage and wondered if that whore of a stewardess next door was around. Sometimes she wore a red uniform and other times a yellow one. Sometimes he would see her going in, sometimes going out. Once he had even stared at her, but she wouldn't look at him. He knew what she thought: that he was a stupid, poor, low-caste provincial boy with a shit job and no future. Nobody she wanted to be seen with. Just because she flew in jet planes, she thought she was better than him. He wondered if he could find a way to hide a mini-cam in her bathroom while she was away and then watch her strip and take a shower whenever he wanted. That would be killer. He'd already photographed her several times leaving the building, even followed her to the taxi-stand once. He knew she was teasing him because she always walked past the *dhaba* where he went. One day, he was going to travel on an aeroplane, First Class, and she was going to serve him, and maybe he would even be able to talk her into meeting him in the bathroom and they would join the Mile High Club together, like he had read online. The website had said stewardesses did that all the time. He would think about that later. He turned the handle and slowly pushed the door open.

Hari Bhaiyya scurried up to the small front-facing conference room on the third floor, where the three goddesses were still seated at the table, finishing their meeting, and said, "Adita madam must come with me at once. You must not take your taxi. Quickly, the back stairs to the roof."

"I don't understand," Adita said, but she sensed an unmistakable urgency in Hari Bhaiyya's request. It was clear to all three that she needed to heed his words and they began to pack up their possessions quickly.

"I'm not leaving you alone," said Harpreet. "Whatever is happening, we stick together. Hari, tell us what's going on."

"Yes, whatever it is, I'm coming with you too," Shoba said.

"Ladies will come with me first," Hari Bhaiyya said. "Then I will tell."

Hari Bhaiyya led them through the deserted office cubicles, up the back stairs, past the small area where he slept and cooked, and to the roof. They now stood in the ochre dusk, overlooking the southwest corner of Electronic City. Across a trash-covered ditch, beyond a row of trees, they could see a cluster of gigantic satellite dishes, and buildings old and new, and construction sites and cranes and towers. A light breeze was blowing, and the three young women moved to a bench that sat along a wall and waited for Hari Bhaiyya's explanation.

"Adita madam's father is here," Hari Bhaiyya said. "With a tough young man who stands behind him like a gangster. He has probably filed a complaint with the police. Two constables are with him, and also an ASI who has a gun. Your father wants to meet Ricky sir. I have them in the basement canteen. I did not want you walking out to the taxi, what with the possibility of him seeing you. You understand?"

Adita clasped Shoba's arm, who sat to her right. "My goodness, Hari Bhaiyya," she said. "Of course you did the right thing. Does Ravi know?"

"Nobody knows yet," Hari Bhaiyya said. "Except for the few people who saw them walk to the canteen, and the security guards. I left two of our guards with them. Now I need to tell Ricky sir. Do you want me to get Ravi?"

"Let me SMS him," Adita said. "I'll have him meet me up here. *Pitaji* wouldn't recognise him if he walked by. Ravi and I need to talk this over. You can go and tell Ricky Sir where we are. Also, be careful: the young man with my father has to be my cousin, and he has a history of violence. Don't let the security guards push him, Bhaiyya. He can be dangerous."

"One has that impression," Hari Bhaiyya said. "I am worried about the police, too. That ASI has a mean expression on his face."

"*Pitaji* must have called his Brigadier friend back home who knows many people in Delhi. He seems to have gotten the local authorities involved. Now, what am I going to do?"

"Don't worry, let me speak to Ricky sir. He will know what action to take," Hari reassured Adita. "Luckily, the workday is over, so the building is empty. Imagine the scandal if it had been noon." With this, Hari Bhaiyya headed back down the stairs. As he passed the second floor, his mobile phone rang again.

"Security Guard #8 Raheem, Hari Bhaiyya. Can you please come down to the entrance again? We have more uninvited visitors."

"Who is it? Do you know?"

"It is Nitin sir and his father. But Nitin sir resigned today and no longer has his identity card. His father wishes a meeting with Ricky Talsera sir."

"Hold them there for me," Hari Bhaiyya said. "And sign them in as guests."

Hari Bhaiyya walked down the muddy lane to Building 1 as fast as he could without running. He waved to the security guards who knew him very well, went through the foyer, made a hard left, quickly climbed the stairs and made another hard left turn. He took a deep breath and knocked at the unmarked door which led to Ricky Talsera's office. Seconds later, Ricky himself opened the door.

"Hari?" he said, surprised. "To what do I owe the pleasure? Come in. Why are you out of breath?"

"Two visitors have arrived," Hari Bhaiyya said. "No appointments! I came over immediately. Both of them need to meet you. I am sorry, they gave no warning. Both of them are important and only you can talk to them!" Ricky Talsera regarded him curiously. "They are two parents. Come to talk about their children."

"Whose parents?"

"Adita's. You know her story, right? She loves Ravi, but her father, Raj Kumarji, has selected another boy for her. He's come all the way from Rajasthan to take his daughter home. He is here with his tough nephew, an ASI and two police constables. I have two of our guards with them, down in the canteen. Served them tea. About Adita's father, you have to remember that in his village he is an important man. He is accustomed to respect. You had better see him first. In fact you should go there immediately and welcome him. He is not used to waiting. His nephew is clearly a bit of a thug and those policemen are acting impatient."

"Where is Adita?"

"She is hidden on the roof of Building 3 with her friends Shoba and Harpreet. They are calling Ravi up there too. You should really drop everything and go over to meet her father right now. There's not much time before your other guests arrive for the client meeting."

"You said two parents, Hari. The mother is here, too?"

"No! The other parent is the father of Nitin. Shivani madam made him resign today. I think his father has come to ask for the boy's job back."

I'm not running a software company, Ricky Talsera thought.

I'm running a goddamn counselling centre. "What do you recommend I do, Hari?"

"Meet them. Listen to them," Hari Bhaiyya said. "You don't have a lot of time. But you must listen. Adita's father has come the farthest and waited the longest. See him first."

"Where did you put Nitin's father?"

"Not just the father. Nitin *and* his father. Them I have placed in a small conference room on the second floor."

"I'm going to need a week of vacation after all this," Ricky said. "Okay, I'm ready. Let the fireworks begin."

18

Bananas cradled in one arm, keys in his opposite hand, Shaitan Vikram kicked the apartment door with his toe and it swung open with a low creak. Even before his beady eyes could completely adjust to the dim, he very clearly identified Jaitendra, seated in the swivel chair, waiting for him. "Oh shit," Vikram said flatly, turning towards the entryway, about to make a run for it.

Jaitendra had prepared himself for this. He leapt out of the chair in a flash and tackled Vikram before he could get to the door. Quite a struggle ensued, with Vikram trying to wriggle away as Jaitendra worked to subdue him, no blood drawn. The kid is adrenalin-charged, Jaitendra thought as he rolled over on to his side and Vikram quickly scrambled to his feet. But a figure appeared in the doorway, Neha, with some papers held in her left hand and a small, two-tone plastic device about the size of an electric shaver in her right. She put her arm out and casually zapped Vikram on the upper shoulder. Instantly Vikram froze in pain, shook like a break-dancer and then dropped to the floor, dazed. Jaitendra got up, dragged him to the centre of the room and shut the door.

"Thanks for that. Give me a minute to restrain him," he said simply, grabbing a roll of black plastic electrical tape. "May put up a fight when he comes to."

"Figured there would be trouble," she said. Neha pocketed her personal TaserLady Model 2010, strolled over to the HP printer and grabbed the printout of the supine Nordic woman which rested in the paper tray, studying it only briefly. She looked around the dark lair and its shabby disarray and said, "Nice. First class."

Jaitendra bound Vikram's wrists and easily lifted him into one of the folding chairs. He had just finished taping his ankles when Vikram started to come around. Neha walked to the chair and stood over Vikram, a perturbed expression on her face.

"You had no right to do that," he whimpered. "I'm in pain, I might have brain damage."

Neha hurled the papers at him, and they fell around him on the floor in a random arc. Porn images of white women with big boobs. "I've been saving up all your mail, waiting to return it to you, you creep. Slipping this crap under my door every day. You thought I wouldn't come to know it was you? Something wrong with Indian girls? We're not beautiful enough for you?"

"Brain damage," Vikram repeated. "Need a doctor."

"Grow up, Vikram," Neha said. "That was the lowest setting. You're not gonna die."

"What do you guys want? What are you doing here?"

"Look who is talking," Jaitendra said.

"I don't understand any of this," Vikram said.

"Mind if I have a banana?" Neha asked. She picked one off

the bunch which lay on the floor and started to peel it. "You want one?" Jaitendra shook his head.

"Maybe I should just let her have a go at you first," Jaitendra said. "Unless you are willing to explain your plan for Talsera."

"Plan?" Vikram said. "What plan?"

"Let me zap him again," Neha said. "That'll make him talk."

"Wait! I have information that Talsera will find useful! I have collected much data, I can give you *the competitive edge*, as Conrad Epstein calls it!" Vikram said. "I have loads of insider information."

"I like how he suddenly turns lucid," Neha said.

Vikram stared at Jaitendra, who had swung back to the computer screens. He was systematically starting to reformat the drives. "I have money," Vikram said to his back. "US dollars. A lot of money."

Jaitendra swiveled around, reached into his coat pocket, held up the packet he had found taped under the keyboard. "You mean this money?" Vikram's tiny eyes opened wide.

"We could be partners," he gasped. "Start a company, blow everybody away. I know how. But don't do that to my machines!"

"I am reformatting their drives," Jaitendra said. "You won't be needing this shit."

"Wait! Not that stuff! That is important work. My work! I own it. You are violating my copyright, my intellectual property!"

Jaitendra continued wiping the hard drives clean. The poetical music of keystrokes filled the space. On the three screens, windows rose and fell. Little boxes appeared, asking whether he was sure he really wanted to continue. Yes, he did. Whole universes of data were rendered into nothing and died forever. Jaitendra admired the beauty and the perfection of software. It was like composing music or playing an instrument, like drawing a line or carving in stone. There was a world of unknowable order, a spiritual, mystical dimension to it that he could barely describe. "Vikram," he asked, halting his interaction with the screens, "did you ever think about using your brain to help other people?"

"Who did anything for me, ever?" Vikram said.

"My heart bleeds for this guy," Neha said. "I wouldn't advise you to go into business with him."

Jaitendra found his way into Talsera's intranet which was already open on the right-hand screen, called up Vikram's HR files and started reading the postings. Neha walked over and stood behind him, putting her hand gently on his shoulder. Nobody spoke. In the tiny two-inch square window tucked on the middle screen near the top, the obese Romanian woman, unobserved by anyone, continued to repeat her jiggling dance in an endless, choppy film loop.

When Danny was escorted into Subinspector Singh's office, his host simply motioned to the chair facing the desk. Khaneja didn't say anything either; he plopped down, took out his phone and dialed a number. "Mr. Hooda?" he said. "Dilbar Khaneja here . . . I'm at the Jama Masjid police *thana* and ready for my guest. May I ask you to call Subinspectorji? . . . Thank you, sir."

Within moments, the policeman's mobile buzzed. He picked it up slowly. "Sir," he said warily, and listened for five seconds. "Yes, sir, thank you, sir." He hit the red button, looked at Khaneja, put DeVries's shoes, jacket, belt and the envelope of his possessions on the desk top. Khaneja opened the envelope and examined the objects which spilled out.

"I would like to see the police report," he said.

Subinspector Singh passed over a white paper.

"Both copies," Khaneja said. Subinspector Singh handed over the yellow original. Khaneja took his time reading it. He inventoried everything on the desk. He remembered the film he had luckily got of Lateef planting drugs in DeVries's pocket. He remembered the snapshot of Lateef meeting with Subinspector Singh before DeVries's arrest. He would only bring them out if necessary. "So, let's deal with this alleged drug charge," he said. "I see 'suspicion of possession of dangerous substances,' but there's no evidence bag."

"This must be an error," Subinspector Singh said. "You know how it is, how overburdened the staff gets. Probably somebody writing down lines intended for another report, switched papers in his confusion. There will be no drugs charge."

"Excellent," Khaneja said. "So, as far as we know, no crime was committed by my client."

"Absolutely not," Subinspector Singh said. "To our good knowledge, no crime was committed. An unfortunate misunderstanding."

"I also see listed on the inventory 'a folded paper of handwritten notes.' I will need to see it."

"There is no such paper among the effects?" Singh asked incredulously. "That cannot be!"

"Perhaps it dropped to the floor accidentally?" Khaneja suggested. "You might want to check around your desk, just in case."

Singh began to look around the stacks of documents on his desktop, apparently unsuccessfully. He studied Khaneja's face, which remained impassive. "Mr. Hooda would certainly be grateful if this piece of evidence could be recovered," Khaneja said as he held up his camera screen and showed Subinspector Singh the photograph of Vikram passing the note to DeVries. "Mr Hooda knows our client received such a paper just before his arrest."

At this, Subinspector Singh reached under his blotter, produced the folded note and slid it across the desk. "Obviously an innocent oversight on someone's part," he offered, as Khaneja studied it, nodded and put it away.

"It does occur to me that as no crime was committed, these are unnecessary," Khaneja said, ripping the police report pages in half, then in quarters, then eighths, and then pocketing the pieces. He took out his wallet, and counted out ten thousand rupees in ten large notes. "But it is also clear that some of the state's resources were inadvertently used. Restitution is customary, so I hope this will, in some way, compensate." The notes disappeared from the desktop. "And that this whole incident will be soon forgotten."

"Of course. And I trust you will tell Mr Hooda you had the full cooperation of this unit," Singh said. "If I can be of any further help . . ."

"Yes, can you send for the foreigner DeVries immediately? Let me take him off your hands, out of your responsibility."

After finishing his second cup of tea, which was nowhere as good as the tea served in his village, Raj Kumarji began to feel the symptoms of impatience. However, he knew he had best keep his opinions in check, at least for the moment. He stared across the table at Mahesh, who seemed transfixed by the windowed chamber across the canteen, the one with the sign 'Xbox Room,' where three large screens were mounted on the wall facing a row of easy chairs. Nobody occupied the room, though the screens displayed scorecards and realistic animations of auto chases through modern city streets. Though Raj Kumarji did not know what precisely an Xbox was, he assumed it had something to do with wasting time. The two police constables stared at the room, equally mesmerised. Off to the side, the ASI was muttering into his mobile phone, his eyes darting around the room suspiciously as he spoke.

Raj Kumarji now looked impatiently at the staircase where Hari Bhaiyya had disappeared after serving them tea. He had asked to see the owner, and he would soon settle this matter of Adita's corruption by the big city and the irresponsible conduct of Talsera with him. He had been assured when she was hired, that the girls were always strictly chaperoned, but he now knew that the contrary was true: it was no different in this place; susceptible young women were as likely to be victimised by fortune hunters here as anywhere else.

Finally Hari Bhaiyya reappeared, accompanied by a younger man in casual clothing, wearing sports shoes. Beware of smiling men approaching you with *namaste*, Raj Kumarji thought. This was probably some lesser security chief or administrator or small manager or someone's nephew, whereas he had specifically asked for the owner.

Jaitendra read Vikram's HR file with a detached interest. He wished he'd had the time to do it before the shit had hit the fan, because it explained a lot. It also suggested a way to deal with him now that he had been unmasked: *Parents deceased; four sisters, all married. Everyone raised in his uncle's home, who had kids of his own. College scores excellent. Hired straight out of college. The drinking incident at the party. His mentor asks to be reassigned. Lots of conflict with Shivani. The famous San Francisco trip, which nobody seemed to recognise for its ambition, let alone its sheer audacity.*

"Nobody may have done much for you in the past. But I'd say a lot of people put their trust in you at Talsera from the first day," Jaitendra said. "We try and make everyone feel at home. You owe some people apologies."

"Good luck," Neha said from behind his shoulder. "You think he understands the principle?"

"What are you guys talking about?" Vikram said.

"I rest my case," Neha said.

"You could be right," Jaitendra said. "Maybe it's easier for Vikram to just disappear."

"You wouldn't do that," Vikram said.

"Seems like less handling to me. You see, all events have consequences, something which you seem to ignore. This would be a major karmic lesson for you."

"I can't listen to any more of this," Neha said. "I have stuff to take care of. But before I go, *you*," she said, pointing at Vikram, "are a lout. I don't give a shit about what happens to you. You stay away from me and here's a free piece of advice: do whatever *he* says." With this, she kissed Jaitendra's cheek, and left them alone in the flat.

"That girl likes you," Vikram said, squirming uncomfortably against the flimsy folding chair to which he had been expertly fastened.

"You can delete that from your memory," Jaitendra said. "Let's start talking real business now. You realise a lot of people are mad at you? Not only the people at Talsera, but also that Dutch man. I bet he's a tough one."

"No," Vikram said. "I can handle him. Let me handle him."

"You've offended Ajit Hooda."

"Who is he?"

"Ajit Hooda runs Old Delhi, Jama Masjid. He's aware of everything that goes on there. After you left Karim's, the Dutch man got arrested."

"But I wasn't responsible—"

"You were certainly involved, and it caused Mr Hooda some discomfort. It's a simple choice, Vikram. Either you do the right thing now, or you don't. I'm your new best friend. You have about an hour, there's not a moment to be lost. So we'd better get started."

"I have to use the toilet," Vikram said.

URGENT BLOGPOST FROM KNIGHTTURING

To all my faithful readers. This will be my final post to you. I owe everybody a big apology. I was completely wrong about that company I called Areslat. It is a super company, and people should do business with it. I was being given incorrect information which I irresponsibly passed along. I have now deleted all my prior posts. I deeply regret any inconvenience caused. Please forgive me. Goodbye.

"I like the way that reads," Jaitendra said. "Contrite, to the point, and self-effacing, ha ha!"

"I still need to use the toilet," Vikram said.

"What do you say we also shut down these windows with the dancing woman and this Korean lady and this alleged fifteen-year-old from Sao Paolo? She looks a bit older than fifteen to me."

"Please sir, save the woman from Brazil. I really like her. We have been having chatting dates."

Jaitendra frowned. "Goodbye Romania," he said, and the window disappeared. "Adios, Korea," he said, clicked the X, and the IM box evaporated. "Let's hang on to South America for another few minutes and say bye-bye to all the gambling and games first. I moved all the porn to the trash. Next step: the Talsera intranet. I'm going to work on this for a few minutes by myself—turn off your access to the surveillance cameras, lock you out, close a few holes. So, sit back and relax."

"But leave the Brazilian girl, sir, please," Vikram said. "And the toilet, sir, please, this is an emergency, Jaitendra sir!"

19

Jan DeVries, his arrogance undiminished, was brought down from the holding room on Subinspector Singh's orders. "You took your sweet time," he said to Khaneja, as he entered the room. "I intend to press charges and report this so-called policeman. He is a menace to society."

"Take a look at your valuables first, and make sure everything is there. The Subinspector has graciously offered you the use of his private bathroom if you want to clean up a bit and reassemble yourself before we get you back to Gurgaon."

"I am going to make more trouble for you than you can imagine," DeVries said, turning to face Subinspector Singh.

"*Mijnheer, Ik raad u aan om meteen uw bek te houden,*" Khaneja said. "The Subinspector explains that you inadvertently wandered into a police operation in progress, and events flew out of control. He has agreed to withdraw all charges and release you immediately. No report will be filed."

"You are free to go, with our apologies," Subinspector Singh said, wobbling his head. "You should never have strayed into Old

Delhi by yourself, sir. Next time, you will know to take someone with you."

"There was this matter of a small administrative charge, but that too has been taken care of," Khaneja added.

"Yes, you are free to go," Subinspector Singh repeated. "Do you understand? Now you may leave."

"And what about that low-life who offered me drugs? Shouldn't something happen to him?"

"He was an informant involved in a sting who got overexcited," the Subinspector said. "He will be dealt with."

"Where's this private bathroom?" DeVries asked in exasperation, grabbing at his possessions, even as he held his casual trousers up at the waist. Singh pointed to an unmarked door. It was surprisingly clean, modern and white-tiled, with a chair and open counter space. A fresh bar of jade green Medimix soap sat perfectly squared to the corner of the basin. He searched furtively for the folded paper Vikram had handed him in Karim's, but it was nowhere to be found. He powered up his Vertu phone—35 messages, most of them from Shivani. He wondered where she was and how much she knew. Her last message read:

DON'T SAY ANYTHING

He turned on the water and washed his face for the first time in hours.

Meanwhile, Khaneja said to Subinspector Singh, "You will find a small gesture of respect for Ajit Hooda, some useful technology. Wait about two hours, and send half a dozen men to Dwarka Sector 6, DDA flats. Block C, number 512A. It's a fifth-floor corner flat. The door will be open. Take whatever you want from the place."

Moments later Jan DeVries reappeared, somewhat put-together. "Well?" he said. "Are we leaving or aren't we?" He opened the door to freedom and looked back. "You go first," he said to Khaneja.

Khaneja led the entire way back to the Jama Masjid parking area. DeVries attempted to speak once, but Danny shook his head. "First we get you out of this place, and then we talk."

When they got to Khaneja's car, DeVries stopped again. "I had a driver here this afternoon."

"He's gone back," Khaneja said. "I took care of that already. He doesn't know anything."

"How'd you figure out where I was?"

"Mr DeVries, I am playing on my home field. Do you have any idea how much trouble you were in? There were a lot of big ifs at play here. If you hadn't gone to meet that guy, if I hadn't been looking for you, if I didn't have a contact with a local politician, if I didn't know how these things work . . . . I mean you are so out of your league."

Minutes passed, stony silence. Khaneja piloted his car over to Connaught Place, turned in the direction of Dhaula Kuan, then got on the expressway to the airport and drove through the tag lane at the toll.

"You didn't see a folded paper among my effects, did you?" DeVries asked out of the blue. "Some handwritten notes, jottings, nothing of consequence." Khaneja didn't reply and drove on for another few miles, not watching his speed. It was ninety kilometres

186

per hour. Just before Mahipalpur, a cop hiding behind some bushes stepped out holding his speed gun and flagged Khaneja down, into a line of ten cars waiting along the shoulder of the road.

"I can't believe I am going to be *challaned* now," Khaneja said. "Perfect timing." He stopped the car, put his hands on the wheel and dropped his head forward.

"What's happening?" DeVries said. "Why are we in this queue?"

"Karma," Khaneja said, twisting in the seat. "Yours or mine, I don't know which. But since we're going to be here a while, let's get a few things straight. First, look at this picture, you and Vikram meeting at Karim's. Are you aware this is an ex-Talsera employee operating illegally in direct violation of a non-solicitation letter?" He held up his phone so DeVries could see the screen. "And here's a photo of him passing you a sheet of paper."

"This is outrageous," DeVries said. "You've been following me, snooping around."

"Here's what's on the sheet of paper," Khaneja said, showing him a photo of the document. "Looks like Vikram's handwriting to me. I call that sabotage. And also shooting yourself in your own foot. The document's been sent to my home office and our people are already on the case. Your little conspiracy is worthless now. You've been caught red-handed. Vikram is already offline. Now you decide how you want to play it. Are you going to cooperate or are you going to go down in flames? Do you want people to know how you came by that incriminating paper?" DeVries said nothing. He looked at the traffic streaming by, and Khaneja's earnest face. "Or is this something you and Shivani are plotting?" Khaneja asked him.

"You leave Shivani out of this."

"No. I need to know your game with her. If you guys have been colluding, I want to know, because then she hasn't been telling us everything either. And by the way, you owe me a couple of hundred euros. I made that police report go away. You can't imagine what it would have cost if they had filed charges. You'd have been stuck here for a month or two at least. Why don't you pay me in cash, right now, before we do anything else? And then look in the glove box and grab me the papers for my car. I have to go see that cop. And while I work things out with him, why don't you think about what you want to tell me?"

Jan DeVries exhaled slowly. "I didn't know you spoke Flemish," he said.

The man welcomed him with a *namaste* and inquired as to the voyage; observed that Raj Kumarji must have traveled many miles. Raj Kumarji said that that was none of his business. Then he asked if tea had been served and if the gentleman wanted something to eat. Before Raj Kumarji could protest, Ricky ordered Hari Bhaiyya to bring a plate of samosas, but Raj Kumarji would have no more of it.

"I am not here to exchange pleasantries, young man. So let's do away with the false politeness. I am here for my daughter. Please get her at once so that we can leave."

"But, sir—" Ricky attempted.

"No, I do not want to listen to anything," Raj Kumarji interrupted forcefully, narrowing his eyes, the compulsive twitch at the side of his mouth now more pronounced. "I have come all the way to Delhi to deal with this in person. I was led to believe that this was a reputable company. I would never have allowed my daughter to accept employment here if I knew you also employ fortune-hunters. She was a simple girl but she has become entangled with a rogue who has seduced her. Young man, the honour of my family is threatened and I will do whatever it takes to defend it. Also, I had asked to see the owner of the company, not some junior employee in jeans and sport shoes."

Hari Bhaiyya spoke up. "Raj Kumarji, this is Ricky Talsera, he is one of the owners."

"You are owner of this company?"

"I and two partners," Ricky admitted. "And, sir, we take the welfare of our team very seriously. I can assure you—"

"You are the owner," Raj Kumarji repeated, sizing up Ricky from head to toe.

"They call me the Managing Partner," Ricky said.

"And you encourage your employees to romance at the workplace and run wild? What kind of an office is this?" Raj Kumarji said, his irritation mounting. "Listen, this conversation is over. Please get my daughter immediately. I am taking her home."

"But, sir, would you consider hearing our side of the story?"

"I would not!" Raj Kumarji shouted. "I am warning you. Get me my daughter or—"

ASI Thakur interrupted. "I believe that is a good idea," he said to Ricky. "Let us settle this in a civilised way. I do not want to have any more discussion. This father has come to collect his daughter and it is getting late. They have a long trip home. Where is the girl?"

Ricky Talsera looked at Hari Bhaiyya, who blurted out, "She is in the building."

"But won't you at least listen to our side of the story?" Ricky made a final attempt.

"No," Raj Kumarji said. "I just want to see the girl, and I want to see her right now."

"In that case, you will have our full cooperation. Hari Bhaiyya, where is she?" Ricky said.

"She is on the terrace," Hari Bhaiyya said reluctantly.

"Good. Let's go there," Raj Kumarji said, standing up. He nodded to his nephew and then the constables.

Hari Bhaiyya led the group up the stairs. It was a strange procession, Hari Bhaiyya in the lead, followed by Raj Kumarji, Ricky, and then the ASI. The constables and security guards clambered after. Up the winding staircase they went, to the third floor landing, across the open plan office of empty cubicles, to the back staircase, passing Hari's sleeping cubby, arriving at the door to the roof terrace. There Hari stopped, and allowed all the men to catch up before he opened the door.

Outside on the terrace, Ravi tried to calm Adita. He had received her SMS when he was in the TT room of Building 2, where he was waiting with the three Patel brothers for a fresh helping of idli that the kitchen was preparing. They had rushed over as soon as her SMS had arrived. Adita had texted

Father is here! Meet me on roof Bldg 3 immdtly

Together they did not make for a threatening lot- the oldest brother was an opera fanatic, the middle brother was a chess grand master and the youngest spent most of his free time in the

Xbox room. But they were Ravi's closest friends and had instantly declared that they would accompany him. Ravi sensed that he might require their help, so he did not protest.

Ravi, holding Adita's hand, suggested that he go down to the canteen and talk directly to her father.

"No!" Adita said. "You don't know what a gangster my cousin is. Please don't—"

Just then, the staircase door burst open and a procession of men, led by Hari Bhaiyya, stormed onto the roof.

Raj Kumarji took immediate note of the clean-cut boy who held his daughter's hand and sat next to her on a bench. He motioned to his nephew, who immediately rushed forward to push Ravi aside and grab his cousin. But the Patel brothers shuffled in between and a confused scuffle began between the nephew and Ravi's friends who were unaccustomed to fistcuffs of any sort. In no time, two of the Patels were down on the ground. But the third managed to tackle Mahesh and now struggled with him on the concrete rooftop.

Shoba and Harpreet leapt forward, screaming at the nephew to leave them alone. The two Talsera security guards joined the fracas and tried to separate the Patels from the nephew. Hari Bhaiyya, Ricky and ASI Thakur held back at the doorway, watching the situation unfold, unsure of how to intervene.

Raj Kumarji had seen enough. He pushed aside everyone and tried to reach Adita, but again the Patels interceded. Mahesh broke free from the Talsera guards and leapt at Ravi, who had stood up with his hands upraised in a conciliatory gesture, and they fell together to the edge of roof, where Mahesh held Ravi's head over the four-storey drop.

"Ravi!" Adita cried, rushing to his aid, but she was prevented from helping him by the police constables, who stepped between her and the two wrestling boys. One of the Patel brothers grabbed Mahesh by his feet, trying to pull him away from the precipice. Mahesh jumped up, and looked in the direction of Raj Kumarji for instructions. Ravi stood up and dusted off his jeans.

"Get her, you fool!" Raj Kumarji shouted, pointing at Adita.

Mahesh ran towards his cousin but Shoba and Harpreet squared off against him, and he had to back off as he did not want to risk being slapped by two obviously pissed off girls. Two of the Patel brothers saw Raj Kumarji heading for Ravi, and they grabbed him by the arms and kept him back. Raj Kumarji struggled, but the Patel brothers held him fast.

"No! Let him go!" Ravi ordered the brothers, who released Raj Kumarji then.

Mahesh sensed an opportunity and leapt at Ravi. The two fell to the ground again, wrestling at the parapet. The constables looked at ASI Thakur, who tried to make sense of who was who. Which of the three girls was the daughter? Which was the boy? Who were all these other people?

"Hold him while I get my daughter!" Raj Kumarji ordered Mahesh.

By the doorway, Ricky Talsera and ASI Thakur studiously ignored each other and watched Ravi continue to struggle with Mahesh. Raj Kumarji stood over the boys, barking commands, "Grab his arm! Knock him on the head!" he cried.

Adita watched the brawl in progress. "Stop it, Mahesh!" she screamed at her cousin, who now held Ravi in a headlock

"Don't let that boy go!" Raj Kumarji shouted to his nephew.

By this time, Hari Bhaiyya had moved over to the area where the altercation was in progress, and he told the security guards to remove the Patel brothers. Ravi continued to writhe around with Mahesh, and the two constables decided they had better separate the girls, so they attempted to move Adita, Harpreet and Shoba off to the side.

Over by the door, Ricky Talsera stepped next to ASI Thakur. "Tell me how much baksheesh and let's solve this problem," he said.

ASI Thakur had already made his calculations and was ready for the question. "I think fifty thousand ought to do it," he said.

Ricky looked at Ravi and the nephew still going at it. It definitely looked like the nephew was losing some ground. "Twenty thousand," he said.

"*Theek hai*," ASI Thakur said. Ricky took out his wallet and handed the amount to him. At that exact moment, Ravi gained a momentary advantage, a strange balletic somersault occurred, and Mahesh went over the side of the building with a grunt. All the action stopped. Ravi stood up, a surprised look on his face, and walked to the parapet. He looked down.

The others also rushed to the edge, where they stood in a line and looked down at Mahesh. He was sprawled out among the solar panels.

"Have you had enough excitement, *Pitaji*?" Adita shouted at her father.

Hari Bhaiyya ran towards the door and the others rushed after him. He led the whole group down to the lower floor and out to the shallow terrace which had broken Mahesh's fall.

As soon as Khaneja climbed out of the car, Jan DeVries got on the phone to Shivani. She didn't even say hello.

"Where the hell are you?" she screamed. "Still in jail?"

"No. That was all a misunderstanding," DeVries said. "All cleared up now. I'm on my way back to my hotel in Khaneja's car, but we've stopped next to a big airfield or something. Why don't you meet me in the bar around midnight? We'll have a drink—"

"Not so fast. First tell me—what's this shit about you meeting Vikram?"

"Who's Vikram? Oh, you mean that kid who was trying to con me?"

"You never mentioned anything about it to me."

"I didn't take it seriously."

"You took it seriously enough to meet him at Karim's."

"I was trying to find out how much he knew. I walked into the middle of some drug sting, and your friend Khaneja bailed me out."

"He let them press charges?"

DeVries chuckled. "Not a chance. We bribed somebody and the whole thing went away. So what about it, Shiv, want to meet me at my hotel later? I'd need a bath and a power nap first; then we could hook up for a midnight dinner. What say?"

"You don't know anything more about what Vikram was up to?"

"Shivani, it was the first time I was setting eyes on the guy. How could I know I was dealing with a delusional nerd? You can't make out who is what on the internet."

"I better not get any more surprises," she said. "Or you're gonna get in some big trouble."

"I'm betting we hook up in the Seychelles. Whoa, Khaneja's coming. He must have solved his problem."

"Well, I have a meeting to attend down here. I'll check in with you after it. Bye." And she hung up.

"Remember our deal," Jaitendra said to Shaitan Vikram. "You keep your mouth shut all the way to the car, no matter what I do. You say a word and I will break your jaw. Clear?"

"Clear," Vikram said.

The Nigerian had been lingering below, near the intersection of the paths, but when they started down the stairs, he scurried across the plaza and walked into the shadows at the far side. Jaitendra walked right over to him, dragging Vikram along, occasionally grabbing his shirt front and yanking him forward, and halted in front of the doorway where he could see the Nigerian hiding, smoking his cigarette.

"We're leaving now," Jaitendra told the shadowy figure. "I'm taking this gentleman for a little ride; you're welcome to try and follow us. But I'm going to do everything in my power to lose you. Don't try anything stupid, or endanger any innocent people. Or you answer to me."

The Nigerian never left the shadows, just smoked and listened. When Jaitendra fired up his car, he saw the Nigerian in the rearview mirror, pulling his own vehicle into the street behind them, in cool pursuit.

"So you remember our deal?" Vikram said.

"Of course I remember. If I say I'll do it, I will," Jaitendra said. "But you have to do your part first."

"If I do it, I get the money and the girl. Right?"

"That's right. But only after you deliver on your promise."

"The money," Vikram said. "And the girl."

"Correct."

From her apartment window, Neha watched them drive away. He had given her specific instructions, and one of them was to get out of her apartment as fast as she could. Neha packed her case, but she didn't wear one of her uniforms. She looked around the flat, wondering when she would next see it. She made sure everything was put away, locked the door and set off for the taxi stand in her sports shoes, dragging her rolling bag behind her.

20

"What finally happened with Raj Kumarji?" Ricky asked Hari Bhaiyya.

"The assistant sub-inspector had a private word with him, but I think the old man had already changed his mind about Ravi by then."

"The kid put up quite a fight for the girl. And remember how he ordered his friends to release her father in the middle of the fight?" Ricky said.

"You didn't see it, but when we went down to the solar panels to look at his nephew, Raj Kumarji almost electrocuted himself; Ravi grabbed him before he could turn into a human French fry."

Ricky Talsera laughed. "That Ravi's a pretty decent boy."

"It also helped when Adita told her dad about how much money she had made playing the stock market with her girlfriends. Suddenly her dad doesn't think Talsera is such a bad place for her to work."

"Thank goodness Khaneja-ji immediately sent the boy to Dr. Narayan," Hari Bhaiyya added.

"So what do I need to know about Nitin's father? Is he going to be furious?"

"I don't think so," said Hari Bhaiyya. "He's just going to try and reason with you."

"That won't be necessary," Ricky said. "The kid stays in the company." He looked at his watch. He didn't have much time before the fireworks. "Let's hope it doesn't take too long. I have a full plate tonight."

"I will get him immediately," Hari Bhaiyya said.

Six minutes to pull himself together, Ricky Talsera thought. He wondered what had become of DeVries, and if Jaitendra would be able to bring Vikram back to Gurgaon, and what magic tricks Khaneja had had to perform. And his mind returned to Shaalu, but only for a flickering moment, since Hari Bhaiyya again opened the conference-room door, escorting in a middle-aged man, quite average and mild in appearance, followed by Nitin, unusually docile, his eyes downcast.

"You are Mr. Talseraji?" Nitin's father asked. "I have the pleasure?"

"Welcome," said Ricky. "How can I be of service?"

"My son Nitin was dismissed from your company earlier today, under circumstances which I do not fully understand. If I could get a better picture of what has happened, perhaps we would be able to help Nitin appreciate where he has displeased his employer. Or what he can do better in his next job, that is, if he cannot return to your good graces. Can I know why he was asked to resign so suddenly?"

"She said it was a difference in styles—" Nitin interjected.

"Nitin, please. I am speaking with Mr Talsera-ji, so do not interrupt. Was there a problem with my son's performance on the job, sir? Did he fall short of some goal or quota?"

"Not to my knowledge," Ricky said.

"Did he break some company rule?"

"No, absolutely not," Ricky said. "In fact, Nitin had been working on something very special for us."

"Then what is this difference of style? Is it some term related to computerisation?"

Ricky Talsera smiled. "It is a poor excuse," he said. "Something people use when a good enough reason cannot be given."

"You see," Nitin's father said, "I come to you not only on Nitin's behalf, but on behalf of our whole family. Nitin is the only source of income we have. I retired two years ago, poor health, around the time when he joined your company. His mother does not work. I can't say there's that much left in savings. We depend completely on his salary."

Ricky Talsera watched the man, and he understood how difficult it must have been for him to have asked for such a meeting, to have made such an appeal, to have revealed such details. "Nitin was doing good work for us," he said. "And I heard excellent things about his special project. His resignation came as quite a surprise to me as well. I am prepared to—"

At that very instant, there emanated from the area outside the conference room the noise of a commotion- shouting, first two men, then a woman, scuffling and stumbling about. Then suddenly the door to the conference room was thrust open and Shivani barged in, followed by two hapless security men and

Hari Bhaiyya. "What's *he* doing here?" she demanded, pointing at Nitin. "And who's *he*?" she derisively asked, pointing at Nitin's father. Then she turned towards the security guards and screamed, "You dare touch me!"

"He's Nitin's father," Ricky Talsera said. "And it's alright, Hari Bhaiyya, you can leave us. Just keep the security guards by the door. Nobody leaves or comes in without your approval."

"*Haanji*, sir," said Hari Bhaiyya.

"What are these two doing here?" Shivani repeated. "Nitin resigned this afternoon. End of story. Thanks for coming by, now you can both go home."

"Not quite," Ricky said to Shivani. "Sit down. This was an unofficial termination, and you had no authority to do it. You didn't go through me and also left HR completely out of the loop. And you threw Nitin out while he was in the midst of a confidential project for Rajan. Nitin was almost about to locate the person who broke into our email, the source of those anonymous blogposts that were trashing your own project."

"Sir, I know where they were coming from—" Nitin said.

"You keep out of this," Shivani said.

"Who is this woman?" Nitin's father asked.

"She is Shivani madam," Nitin said, and his father sat up a little straighter and regarded her shrewdly.

"What is so wrong with my son's style that you asked him to resign because of it?" he asked her.

"I can't believe this!" Shivani said, looking at Ricky. "You're going to let some parent come in and tell you how to run your company?"

"Relax, Shivani," Ricky said, exhaling deeply. "This man came to speak on his son's behalf, and I think he has an excellent case for reinstatement. Plus, Nitin had almost nailed the negative blogger."

"Well, we don't need Nitin to tell us that. I've discovered who the blogger was and it's all been taken care of. Is this the kind of thing you want to be discussing with an ex-employee in the room?"

"Nitin, can you provide us with evidence of who the blogger was, where those messages came from and the kind of documentation that might hold up in a court of law?"

"Sure, sir."

"That's ridiculous, Ricky," Shivani said. "I told you I made it all go away. You don't need this boy."

Ricky ignored Shivani and continued to address Nitin. "Good. Now, would you consider returning to work tomorrow and finishing the project for us?" Shivani stared at him, open-mouthed. "And after you're done, would you consider returning to our company as a fulltime employee, like you were before this improper resignation occurred? I will be recommending you for a raise if you successfully complete the project."

"Yes, sir! I can return to work immediately!" Nitin blurted out. "I will have all the necessary documentation for you first thing tomorrow. I will work all night!"

Shivani gave off with an inelegant snort. "Everybody in this place has lost their mind," she said. "Get a grip, Ricky."

"Also, Nitin, Rajan has agreed to mentor you."

"Who is this Rajan?" Nitin's father asked.

"Crazy," Shivani said. "You guys are asking for trouble."

"You are a very odd woman," Nitin's father said. "Why are you so impolite to everyone?"

Shivani stood up. "I'm not taking this," she said.

"Sit down, Shivani," Ricky Talsera said. "You're not going anywhere. We're about to have the RoodInfo status review, and you're hanging around for it. Nitin, I must ask you and your father to leave us alone if our business is settled. And, Shivani, now don't say anything. Nothing."

The traffic cop wanted to *challan* him for a thousand, but Khaneja apologised, said he was in a hurry and asked if he could please the cop in some other way.

"Two hundred," the cop said.

Khaneja handed him a five-hundred-rupee note, got his receipt but no change, and headed back into traffic. The highway was clogged with vehicles flowing in and out of Haryana, every manner of conveyance, and Khaneja wove around broad trucks and smoke-spewing buses and two-wheelers, amidst the unending cacophony of horns.

"Wait a moment," DeVries ventured. "Isn't that my hotel we just passed?"

"It is," Khaneja answered, staring straight ahead.

"So where are we going?"

"To your status review."

"That's absurd. It was cancelled. I want to go to my hotel. I'm not prepared. I've been in a jail all afternoon. You can't just do this to me. I need to bathe, I need to eat, I need to make some calls, some notes."

Khaneja swooped off the flyover, piloting his car down into the melancholy avenues of Gurgaon, and turned left in the direction of the Electronic City. "You can do that later. At the moment, a lot of people want to talk to you. So we're going straight to the office."

An uneasy silence prevailed in the large conference room where Ricky and Shivani waited. The wide plastic vent on the wall-mounted air-conditioner unit moved up and down in its rhythmic way, throwing a stream of cool air over the tabletop. Shivani tapped her lacquered fingernails impatiently for a while. Finally she said, "If you don't mind, I'm gonna check my emails." And she took out her Blackberry and started scrolling.

"Hold on," she said suddenly. "There's a farewell blogpost up from that Knight-touring bastard. He says he deleted all the negative posts about us and that he was wrong about everything. Says he's sorry. A bunch of people have already pinged me about it. I told you I had it under control."

Ricky looked at his watch. Where was Khaneja?

At that exact moment, Khaneja was parking his car outside Building 3. In one sense he was happy it was dark and DeVries couldn't see the surroundings, but then he remembered he did not give a damn about what the Dutchman thought anymore. He'd figured out that Talsera had been the victim of Vikram's duplicity and DeVries's connivance, and he wanted to see where Shivani fit into that nonsense. With luck, she would be in the conference room with Ricky, waiting.

They found Hari Bhaiyya out by the little blockhouse. He

escorted them upstairs, where two security men guarded the door to the big conference room.

"What's with the goons?" Jan DeVries asked. "This is your office building?"

"One of them," Khaneja said. Hari Bhaiyya opened the door, and Ricky Talsera stood up and introduced himself.

"Hello, Shiv," DeVries said. "Nobody told me you were going to be here as well. Ready to clear the air and move forward?"

"Yes," Shivani said. "Let's clear the effing air. What have you been up to? You went out to Old Delhi and you didn't tell me?"

"Personal business—" DeVries attempted.

"Seems Mr DeVries went to Karim's on his own and had a brush with the underworld," Khaneja said.

"I wasn't asking you," Shivani said. "And I want answers now. From everybody here. You first, Khaneja. You tell me what you found out."

Ricky cleared his throat. "I called this meeting, Shivani, so I'll run the discussion from here on. Why don't *you* begin by telling us what you were doing with Mr DeVries at the Radisson, two days running? The barman remembers you and so does the deskman. According to the doorman you two—"

"What business is that of yours?" DeVries said angrily. "What's this got to do with the job?"

"You tell me," Ricky said.

"So you've been spying on me!" Shivani shouted. "This is the thanks I get for bringing in such a big contract? You have no idea what I have had to do to keep this job moving forward."

"Shivani and I are renewing an old friendship," DeVries

said. "Has nothing to do with the project, nothing at all. Strictly extracurricular. As for that kid, *he* solicited me and I just wanted to see what his game was. It did seem he had the juice to deliver what he claimed he could. Look at the havoc he wreaked on your people. Also, I had no idea he was a one-man show until today."

"And how did you figure that out?" Ricky asked.

"I told him," Khaneja said.

"Thanks for telling me," Shivani said. "My client, my account, and you keep me in the dark."

"And you terminate people without going through channels. Do you have any idea what that could have cost us, Shivani?" Ricky said. "Reputation in the job market. That ever crossed your mind?"

"Well, if you don't appreciate the job I'm doing—"

"The client wishes to speak," Jan DeVries said. "Are any of you interested in my opinion? You are? First, Danny Khaneja got me out of that goddamn jail. I don't know how he did it, but I'm thankful for that. Second, those blogposts were an irritant, I never thought much of them in the first place. The fact that somebody has tracked the bad guy down and engineered the retraction is impressive. But the things that the kid pointed out, they concern me still, and I will need to see that your work is bulletproof before we decide whether we want to keep our business with you."

"So you're willing to stay with us," Ricky said.

"If my team checks out the latest updates and they look good, I see no reason to discontinue the relationship for the present," DeVries said, looking at Khaneja.

"Great. And I intend to fully supervise every aspect from now on," Shivani said.

"That won't be necessary," Ricky said. "I think it's time you took a long vacation, Shivani. We'll pay you the commissions, but I want you out of the management loop from now on. Your presence is toxic here. Don't look so shocked. I'm asking for your resignation."

"Yes," Khaneja said. "We have a difference in styles."

"What's that supposed to mean?" Shivani said, narrowing her dark eyes. "I'm not going along with it, Ricky. You can't ask me to leave. I helped build this company. I drove my teams to excellence."

"You are right. *Drove*," Khaneja said. "The definition of wisdom is knowing when to say enough."

"I hate to interrupt your little quarrel," DeVries said, "but none of this concerns me—"

"You shut up," Shivani cried. "I'm staying on the project until it's done, then we will talk about my resignation. And let me assure you, it's gonna cost you. A lot."

"Maybe you *do* need a little vacation, Shivani," Jan DeVries said. "A little trip to a tropical island, a beach? Something to reduce the stress in your life. Looks like these guys can handle things on their own."

Shivani glared at him. "Why're you suddenly *so* cooperative?" she asked. "Wait a minute. I get it. Khaneja has something on you."

21

Perfect, thought Shaitan Vikram, so this is what it has come down to. The Einstein conference room on the second floor of Building 3, Hari outside the door, backed up by two security dudes. Dark outside. Sitting across from me—everybody who ever tried to ruin my professional life.

Jaitendra hadn't made a big scene when he had delivered Vikram to the conference room. He had knocked politely, opened the door slowly, gotten cold stares from everybody at the table, installed Vikram to Ricky's right. Stood in the space between him and Shivani, nodded to Ricky. Said "Man" as a greeting to Danny Khaneja and "Must be the Dutch guy," glancing at Jan DeVries.

"Don't you dare touch me," Shivani warned Jaitendra.

"No, I wouldn't," Jaitendra said. "You may have tantric powers. I think everyone here knows Vikram, yes? I must inform you that Vikram's being very cooperative. He's even willing to tell his side of the story."

"He'd better goddamn well," Shivani muttered. Nobody spoke

207

up, so she went silent, and stared at Vikram. Jan DeVries looked down at the plate of biscuits, took one and nibbled at it.

Vikram sat hunched in his chair. He was just getting back to normal after being tackled by Jaitendra and then shocked by that bitch and then tied to a fucking chair for two hours as he watched his whole universe being deleted.

"I have some questions," Ricky said, looking intently at Vikram. "Start with talking about stolen passwords and how you broke into our firewall," Ricky said.

"Oh, I needed them," Vikram said, beginning to register some enthusiasm. "Needed to watch the video feeds, read the mails, wander around the project looking at what the developers were doing, keep an eye on people at the office, stay on top of who was working. It was easy to mess up RoodInfo, nobody knew I was there. It was perfect. I was like the invisible man."

"You were going to blow up my project from the inside, just to get back at me?" Shivani said.

"No way," Vikram said. "I just wanted you guys to suffer."

"That's pathetic. You ever thought about how illegal this was, you stupid little shit?" Shivani asked. "I could go after you so bad you'd never recover. I can ruin you, you may never get to do business in this industry ever again. Anywhere in the world."

"I was not leaving any tracks, you know," Vikram said, speaking to Ricky and ignoring Shivani. "More like I was working *against* the company, if you get the difference. See, if I could have helped Mr DeVries, then it would have been a win-win situation. I could have made some money, he would have gotten a better deal, and you guys would've learned an important lesson. And it almost worked, didn't it?" His little eyes shifted back and forth from Shivani to Jaitendra to Khaneja and back.

"You could have brought everybody down with those negative blogposts," Khaneja said.

"It's cool now, man. They're all deleted, and I posted a big apology to everyone." He looked at Jaitendra, who nodded.

"Do you have any idea how much trouble you have caused?" DeVries said.

"I'm getting the idea," Vikram said. "I'm very sorry."

"You realise you violated every privacy law known to man?" Shivani said. "That is harsh."

"Harsh," Vikram said. "It is. I am sorry I came off as the bad guy. But you know what, Shivani? You are a big problem all the time as well. You are not a very nice person to other people either."

Shivani shot him a savage look. "Vikram," Jaitendra interrupted, "we would also love to know what really happened in San Francisco. You took those freshers to a gambling parlour?"

Vikram snickered, a sick little smile on his face. "I took them to Reno," he said. "Played blackjack in an important casino, and I won big. We got home before curfew, right under her nose, and nobody came to know." Vikram snickered again, hunched down in the chair.

"That's everything?" Ricky asked. Jaitendra nodded.

"You have a rehab plan for Vikram?" Khaneja asked.

"He and I have a deal. Don't we, Vikram? I had considered terminating him with extreme prejudice."

"I'd vote for that," Shivani said. "I say we throw him into a vat of fresh cement somewhere along the new metro line and forget about him."

"Shivani, you're fired, as of now," Ricky said. "It's an exceptional circumstance for the company, but I've had enough of you. You should leave us right now. Hari will escort you out."

"That was awesome, sir," Vikram said.

"I'm satisfied," DeVries said. "Come on, Shivani, let me buy you a consolation drink. Leave these guys to clean things up. Time to delegate, you understand?"

"Ricky, I put a lot into this. And suddenly I am unwanted?" Shivani asked.

"That's right," Khaneja said. "You had better go."

"There will be lawyers," Shivani said.

"There always are," Khaneja said. "But mine are bigger than yours."

"Somebody's going to pay," she said.

"I'm going to let the next status review happen between you and my staff," DeVries said to no one in particular. "I have complete confidence in you. Now, I hope to be on the first flight out of this place tomorrow morning." Let's get out of here, he motioned to Shivani. Shivani leapt to her feet and stood nose to nose with Jaitendra, but since she was a good six inches shorter than him, she had to rise up on her toes inside her high-heeled black shoes.

"What do you have on him?" she demanded.

Khaneja said, "Shivani, come on."

"If it's the money you are worried about, you'll get your part of it," Ricky said. "We plugged the leaks and kept the account and removed the threat. We'll see the project through and move on to the next. Without you. Don't look at me like that, Shivani. Time to go."

Once the door had closed behind them, Vikram said, "So now, what about me?"

"The deal is on," Jaitendra said to him and then turned to Ricky. "Ricky, I turned off the blog, locked him out of our network and wiped every one of his hard drives clean, even his backup drives. He says he doesn't have any other backups and for once I believe him."

"You erased my best games. All my research, all my projects."

"All your porn and all our proprietary files. I figured a fresh start was needed."

"What is the deal? You're planning to let him go?" Ricky said.

"Yes. The deal goes like this: he comes clean and we give him the chance to start over. He stays out of our business, out of our lives from now on, banished. Right, Vikram?"

"Right," Vikram said. "As far away from you as I can get. As soon as I can."

"And if he ever gets near us again, he understands that I will not be so generous."

"Good," Ricky said. "But Vikram, I don't think you ever understood a simple fact, and I'm not sure you would understand it now but I am going to try and say it anyway. Talsera is not the biggest company in the world, but we are one of the best because we take care of our people. This whole episode tells me you never got that idea. What you almost accomplished would have affected the livelihood of four hundred people. That's the worst part. That's what I lose sleep over. That's the fact you don't seem to understand."

Vikram shrugged. "I guess I'm sorry," he said. "But that kind of makes me a success, doesn't it? I did what had I set out to do. Almost."

"In a perverse way, yes," Khaneja admitted. "But, it's a twisted definition of success, Vikram. It doesn't focus on the greater good for mankind."

"Wait a minute. You're not gonna kill me, are you?"

"I'm going to keep you guessing on that front is what I'm gonna do. Time for you to wait for me down in the car," Jaitendra said and sent a trembling Vikram off with the guards.

Now, only the three men who ran the company were left in the conference room.

"When was the last time we three actually got together like this?" Khaneja wondered aloud. "Just the three of us. We ought to do this more often and also entice Rajan out of his cave. He's missing all this fun."

Jaitendra held up the little white flash drive he had used at Vikram's lair. "I brought back a bunch of Vikram's files. I want you to quarantine the whole lot and put a team of our people on them. Let's see what we learn. Fair's fair, it's our backyard he was playing in. I bet we'd get some good information from it."

"What made the Dutchman turn so agreeable?"

"The list Vikram gave him at Karim's," Khaneja said. "That was another reason why Vikram got so sweet. We have photos of them meeting and of the note being passed. I even got hold of the note. It was a list of all the sabotage he did on the project. You notice neither of them brought it up?"

"That must have been part of your deal with DeVries?" Ricky said. "You never mentioned the sabotage letter earlier."

"Neither did Vikram," Khaneja said. "We made sure of that."

"It's amazing," Jaitendra remarked. "It wasn't the blogposts or the sabotage that did him in. It was an old-fashioned handwritten letter."

As the car rode through the darkened Delhi streets into the centre of the city, Jaitendra ended a call on his mobile phone.

"Is it true that you never took a vacation all these years?" Vikram asked. "They were sure surprised when you asked for some days off. They thought you meant a week. You asked for a month."

"I asked for *at least* a month," Jaitendra corrected him.

"Is it true you killed a bunch of enemy soldiers in Kargil? People say you stormed a hilltop."

Jaitendra didn't acknowledge the question.

"You really are my hero, sir. So where are we going? Can we go out for a beer together? Hang out a little?"

No reply.

There wasn't much traffic on the Aurangzeb Road. They turned down a narrow lane which led to the rear entrance of a huge, walled compound.

EMBAIXADA DO BRASIL
EN NOVA DELHI

"Give me your passport," Jaitendra ordered. Vikram passed it over. A guard carrying a submachine gun opened the gate. He seemed to know Jaitendra because he saluted and said, "Major," motioned them in and closed the gate behind them. Jaitendra counted out $1000 from Vikram's envelope, handed it off with some papers through the window. The guard said, "Be right back, sir," and disappeared from sight. Jaitendra turned the car nose out, so that it pointed to the gate which had closed behind them, and stopped the engine. Then they sat in the orange light and waited.

"There you go," Jaitendra said to Shaitan Vikram. They were outside IGI Terminal 3. "You have a two-year visa and here's your reservation. Let's go inside and buy your ticket now."

"That was awesome at the embassy," Vikram said.

"You owe me on that one. I called in a favour." They walked up to Door C, where an impassive Sikh in an impeccable uniform saluted them.

"Good evening, Major," he said.

"I'm just escorting my friend to the departure gate," Jaitendra said. The Sikh gave Vikram's documents a perfunctory glance and saluted. "Nice to see you, Major," he said, waving them through.

"Awesome," Vikram said.

At the currency exchange counter, Jaitendra counted out $2500, got 100,000 in Indian rupees and the rest in Brazilian reals, which he handed to Vikram. Then they walked to the counter and purchased the ticket to GRU.

"How long is this flight?" Vikram asked.

"Twenty-three hours westbound. You don't need to know eastbound, you're not coming back in a hurry," Jaitendra said. "You change planes in Dubai. Don't leave the airport, you don't have a visa for Dubai. Your layover's not that long anyway. Here's $5000 for spending money. Smart guy like you ought to make that go a long way."

"I hope you bought me a Business Class seat?"

"Economy, Vikram. You need to learn to suffer a little."

"Aw, man, why'd you do that? What about the rest of my money?"

"I've had some expenses: your ticket, your visa, petrol. There's about nine grand left. Let's talk about it in a year, see where you are. If I like what I see, I may pay you back."

"How will you know where I am?"

"I'll find you. You can be sure of that."

"You think that girl is gonna go out with me?"

"An even chance," Jaitendra said. "Women can't be explained, they're running different software. It's kind of up to you what happens next. See you later, Vikram."

The message had come in from the New Delhi boy, one of the several hundred she got every day from guys all over the world. Japanese guys who asked her to send them her used panties. Russian guys who suggested she do the crudest things for the camera, and attached pictures far less beautiful than anything she ever sent. Guys who proposed. Pitiful, lonely guys in shadowy internet cafes from all over the planet. But this message had caught her attention, because this guy had been writing, chatting, joining her Facebook page, liking her on MySpace and pinging endlessly. She had told him she was fifteen, which was six years off, but if he couldn't see the stretch marks in her pictures, that was his problem. She had suggested he send her money to help make the bikini wax video and he had said he would in a few weeks.

Arriving GRU in two days. Can we go out to dinner Thursday night? We can talk about the video. Maybe you can show me the city. My new email and mobile # will follow on arrival.

She couldn't tell if it was real or not, but maybe this guy was actually going to show up and maybe he would be kind and friendly, like it happens in the movies. He may even be The One. She stared across the little room she occupied, at her baby still asleep in the simple crib she had bought. He would be up soon, demand to be fed and she had emails to send. Some man in Athens wanted her to star in his video. A Chinese man wanted her phone number. Lucia, she said to herself, the boy from New Delhi is a much better bet.

22

Ricky and Khaneja, now the only occupants of the conference room, sat at the big table, both somewhat dazed after the many events of the day. A light knock at the door, and Hari Bhaiyya slipped in. "Is everything okay?" he asked.

"Fine," Ricky said. "Taking a breather. Anything more to report about Raj Kumarji?"

"No, all seems well," Hari Bhaiyya replied.

Khaneja's phone rang. He picked it up. "Hello doctor," he said. Paused. Listened. "Yes, yes, just fine, all fine. She is fine. Yes, my son is growing up fast. Yes, I should. Yes, I will. Doc, thanks for admitting the kid. How's he doing? You're releasing him in the morning? You're amazing. And, don't worry about that contribution to the temple. What? Fifty thousand rupees? That's very generous of you. You really don't have to do that." From the tiny earpiece Dr Narayan's distinctive laugh could be heard. Khaneja had to smile. "Doctor, I'm with a couple of friends of yours. May I put you on the speaker? Here goes." He pushed a button and identified Ricky and Hari Bhaiyya.

Dr Narayan loved an audience. He said, "Listen: A guy goes in to see his doctor. The doctor says, 'I've got bad news and terrible news.' Guy says, 'Oh my God, what's the *terrible* news?' Doctor says 'You've got terminal cancer.' Guy says, 'Oh my God! And what's the *bad* news?' Doctor says 'You've also got Alzheimer's.' So the guy says, 'Well, at least I don't have cancer.'"

The joke released some of the tension in the conference room. As the doctor was hanging up, still chuckling at his joke, Ricky Talsera received an SMS. He looked down at the display and scowled. "Priyanka," he said. "I bet it's about that girl and the dog. I don't want to deal with this *now* after everything that just happened."

"I already took care of it," Hari Bhaiyya said. "I spoke to her earlier, told her what I thought the problem was, and Priyanka wanted to see if she could handle it herself. She's an ambitious girl, the kind of person who could take over from you—"

"—in forty years," Khaneja said.

"—so I would advise letting her try handling things like this one all by herself."

"Okay with me," Ricky said, looking down at the SMS.

Ricky I think I have found a resolution for the Pushpa and dog problem. I will report to you late tomorrow. Priyanka (HR)

Danny Khaneja smiled. "Sounds like a self-declared candidate for presidential succession to me," he said.

The Nigerian lurked in the doorway. He kept looking up at the fifth floor, at the corner apartment where Jaitendra had been. Nobody had come back yet. He wondered what was inside the place. Those guys from Talsera had ruined one of Big Boss's coolest schemes ever. He'd almost persuaded some fat-assed Indian industrialist to put sixty crore rupees worth of machinery onto a ship in Kolkata, in exchange for some letters of credit and customs documents, which of course were all brilliant forgeries. Big Boss had given real account numbers, used real letterheads stolen from banks and consulates and had even used the correct seals. But somehow Khaneja, who was advising the industrialist, called up the top guy at the bank and the scam got exposed. The Indian industrialist never put the containers on the ship and Khaneja held on to the bogus documents.

Big Boss sent his boys to get the files back, which they did. But Khaneja found their hideout; the rumour was he had called Ajit Hooda himself to get their location. Later that night, while the boys were out playing cards, Khaneja and Jaitendra broke into the hideout and stole the documents a second time. Big Boss *really* didn't like that and he made the boys miserable for losing the files twice. Then one night when the boys were out drinking beer, the two men from Talsera happened to walk into the same bar.

"You know who we are?" Big Boss asked, never getting up from his seat.

"The losers whose scam wasn't happening," Khaneja said.

Big Boss was not used to getting attitude like that. Two Indians squared off against six Nigerians and the military guy wasn't even armed to the teeth like he was when they had broken into the hideout. But he still turned out to be fierce: he did a wrist grab on the first Nigerian thug, rolled him over with a fist to the chest where he went down, then took care of the second one with a throat grab that sent the guy on to the floor, hacking and clutching his neck—all this in the first thirty seconds. At the same time Khaneja went *mano-a-mano* with a really seasoned tough guy who was an expert with the knife, but even then if Khaneja hadn't caught a slash on his ear, he would have been the winner; not that it mattered because Jaitendra immediately hurled a big Godfather Beer bottle expertly at the assailant and he dropped like a rock. Khaneja then picked up a chair and slammed Nigerian number five. And Jaitendra, wasting not a move, head-butted Nigerian number six into submission. The bar was a battlezone afterwards: broken furniture, shattered glass everywhere and groaning figures on the floor. The Indians got away, and Big Boss said, "From now on we follow those fucking Talsera guys and watch for an opportunity."

Maybe this apartment was finally the opportunity Big Boss was waiting for, the Nigerian thought. He texted the boys and told them to get their butts over to Dwarka *tout de suite*. Right away.

He checked the backpack for his ticket, passport, visa, cash, laptop, phone charger. On his feet he wore his comfy slip-on travelling shoes. Khaneja closed his carry-on bag for the ten thousandth time and looked around his empty apartment. He liked the flat, though they hadn't had much time to work on it. He was always away, and she was with their son the whole day. It was an airy penthouse flat, and if Gurgaon wasn't so polluted, they would have spent more time on its terrace. His wife and son were at her parents' in the country for the week, breathing fresh air, living life at a slow pace. He had another jet to catch, a client to see in Singapore, and some people to drop in on in K-L. It would be another long week on the road—a succession of conference rooms, hotel beds, restaurant food, room service, overpriced laundry, taxis, headsets, duty free shops and late nights drinking whiskey in shadowy bars while dreaming of home. Hari Bhaiyya had told him, "You need to be spending all the time you can with your son now. They don't stay young forever and it passes very fast." Khaneja tried to not think about the boy too much, for he needed to stay focused on the business. Windows closed, lights off, door locked and once again, dear friends, into the elevator, down to the car and back into the sky.

The same two seats at the end of the bar in the Radisson Gurgaon. Midnight. Jan DeVries seated next to Shivani, both sipping their strong drinks. Not a lot of talking. Then a buzz from DeVries's jacket pocket, an SMS. "It's from my office," he said. "They've got me on a 9 a.m. flight to Frankfurt. Guess that means I have about five hours before I need to leave for the airport, right?"

"Yes," Shivani said.

"Guess we'll next meet in the Seychelles in the fall? That is, if you're still up for it."

"I might," she said. "We'll see."

"So, you got anything planned for the next few hours, Shiv? What was the old joke we used to have, a drink—"

"Don't say it," Shivani interrupted him. "Just keep it to yourself."

It was dark and quiet and late in the house. As soon as Ricky opened the door, he inhaled happily, taking in the scents of the place he knew was home. She had left the kitchen light on for him, and a plate of sweets sat on the counter next to the teapot. He knew that in the far corner of the house, his children slept peacefully. These were the tranquil hours when the phone did not ring and the television was silent, the regular business of the family suspended until dawn. He sipped at the cold tea, enjoying the feeling of lightness and familiarity surrounding him. He tiptoed across the living room, stepping over a half-sized red plastic cricket bat that lay in the middle of the rug. On the wall the faces of his ancestors gazed down at him benevolently. He crept along the hallway and hesitated outside his bedroom door in a moment of overwhelming contentment. The door swung open, without his touching it. It was Shaalu, dressed only in her sheer peach Benarsi silk kaftan. The red light bulb in the nightstand lamp illuminated her silhouette through the filmy cloth. Dim light, the bed thrown open, incense burning, a single candle flickering at the altar, setting the marigold shadows aflutter.

Weaving his way through the crowds exiting the arrivals gate, Jaitendra made his way to a car waiting for him outside Terminal 5. It was a black sedan with darkened windows; its driver stood outside and leaned against the boot. When Jaitendra got to him, he opened the door smartly, saluted and said, "Major."

Jaitendra nodded, and ducked into the back seat, where Neha sat. She wore an elegant dove grey silk kurta and churidar, and her hair was braided down her back. She wore a pair of traditional tasteful jootis that suited her attire.

"You certainly took your time," she said.

"I told you it would be at least a couple of hours. You've been here all along? Had any problem finding the driver?"

"No. He has been very nice to me. You told him to take me shopping, no?"

"Correct," Jaitendra said. "And, that's a nice outfit you chose."

"What happened with your friend the little creep?"

"I took him through immigration, then walked him all the way to the departure gate, watched him go aboard and sat there waiting until his plane took off."

"What you guys saw in him I'll never understand."

"You need to hope for the best from people, Neha," Jaitendra said. "He was right. Until Talsera, nobody ever did anything for him."

"Are we still going to that hill station you talked about? The one above Rishikesh?"

"Yes," he said. "It's green and wild and isolated. Let's stay until we can't stand it any longer, and then go someplace else." The car moved gently out of the airport and cruised into the darkness of a long, private road.

"I thought you said we were flying."

"We are," Jaitendra said. "Hitching a ride to Haridwar with a friend. It's a military helicopter, a bit noisy, but it'll be fine." He stared out the window.

"You just got a very bemused look on your face," Neha said. "What's that all about? Share it with me."

Jaitendra turned to her. "I can't wait to see what happens when my mom meets you."

Shaitan Vikram got on the jet for Dubai, found his way to his seat and plopped down. But, suddenly, panic overtook him. He'd only been to one other country besides India in his life—the USA—and that had been easier because he'd seen enough American movies and television to get a hang of things, and also because they spoke something that sounded like English. But already culture shock was setting in, with all the signs and magazines on the plane in Arabic, and all around him women in head scarves, and men with beards. Who knew what Brazil would be like. Firstly, they probably spoke Spanish there, a language which was alien to Vikram. Secondly, he didn't know anybody there, nobody he could call except that girl who wanted to make the video, and she didn't seem too reliable either suddenly. The plane filled up, and Vikram started to hyperventilate. He unbuttoned his collar, tried to breathe deeply. The passenger across the aisle stared at him. Something wrong? Vikram shook his head no, but he couldn't get rid of the dread he felt. There was still a lot of good stuff at the Dwarka apartment. Maybe he ought to go over there and see what he could salvage. Maybe sell it all back for cash at Old Man Banerjee's shop and hide out somewhere else? Hide right under their noses, but stay out of their business. If he didn't get in Jaitendra's way, nobody would know anything.

Vikram stood up impulsively, grabbed his new shoulder bag, the only luggage he had. Jaitendra hadn't even let him pack a suitcase. He'd just bought him the shoulder bag at the airport and told him to buy clothes in Brazil. Vikram ran down the aisle for the exit door and squeezed past the flight attendant. "Panic attack, I'll catch the next flight." He then hid in a jetway alcove until the door behind him closed and he could feel the jet bridge ease away from the aircraft. And, when he was sure the plane had gone and the counter had emptied, he slipped back into the terminal and headed for the exit.

Cradling a bunch of bananas he had purchased, and wondering when the *dhabe* wallah would arrive, Vikram pushed open the unlocked door to his flat, slowly and carefully, and he didn't like what he saw. Three African guys in suits, were playing video games on his screen, and three other guys had set up shop elsewhere in his place. *His* place. They had been drinking beer and smoking bhang. The one in the nicest, shiniest suit looked up at Vikram as if he were some kind of an insect.

"Who the fuck are you?" he asked, pulling out an automatic pistol that did not look friendly at all.

"It's the kid who was working here," one of the other Africans said, in Igbo, a language largely unknown in India, so Vikram had no idea what was said. "I saw Jaitendra take him away hours ago."

"Oh shit—" was all Vikram could muster.

"What are we gonna do with him?" one of the Africans asked.

"Fuck if I know," Big Boss said. "You speak English?" he asked Vikram.

"Yes," Vikram managed to say.

"Got any money?" Big Boss asked. "What's in the bag? Hand it over. Let's see."

Before Shaitan Vikram could do anything more, the door behind him was thrown open with a great crash and suddenly the room was filled with uniformed men carrying automatic weapons, all pointed at Vikram and the Nigerians.

"Drop your weapons," Subinspector Singh said. "You are all under—"

He could never finish the sentence. The Nigerians opened fire, and so did the commandos, and the apartment filled with the sound of gun shots and smoke and the screams of bullets hitting their targets.

The light had grown pastel and dusky, yet it was only 7 a.m. Priyanka waited outside the apartment building. She recalled what she had learned and what she had decided. She had gone out on a limb writing the SMS to Ricky Talsera as she had, but if she was ever going to lead, if ever she was going to have responsibilities like Ricky had, then she realised she would need to take some risks.

At the appropriate moment Pushpa appeared and searched up and down the lane for the cab which came every morning. Instead she caught sight of Priyanka, a girl she knew from Human Resources, standing where the cab usually stopped.

"Come on, Pushpa," Priyanka said, taking her arm not-quite-warmly, leading her in the direction of the busy street. "This morning we're going to take a walk together."

"I don't understand you," Pushpa said.

"You will understand me by the time we reach the cab pickup point."

"But the dog—"

"Stop lying, Pushpa. Two days ago I myself walked the route, unharmed and unbothered."

Pushpa looked from side to side, clearly uncomfortable. "Listen, there *is* a dog," she insisted.

"Oh really? In that case we will say hi to him when we meet him."

They continued silently on the route to the open stretch. Mounds of dirt and piles of rocks covered an overgrown field at their left. Priyanka waved her arm. "Look around. Nobody home."

"I wonder where—"

At that very instant a little runt of a hound, yellow with half an ear, mangy, pint-sized, charged around a hillock and got very close to them. It snarled and barked and jumped and growled in a threatening way. Pushpa panicked and backed off. Priyanka reached into her purse and produced a small canister. Pepper spray. She gave the dog a good shot from it, a poof of mist to the face. Instantly the dog ran off behind the mounds, howling. They heard the sound of its yelping recede as it got blocks and blocks away.

Priyanka looked down. "That was a vicious little bastard," she said.

"I told you," Pushpa said. "The cab better continue to pick me up from home tomorrow onwards."

At approximately the same moment, the sun peered its weary head over the horizon and lit up the ochre particulate matter that hung in the Delhi sky. All over the city homes came alive, and out in the shanty towns, wood fires were built, and people began their morning ablutions. Vendors brought out their wares to set up their modest stalls and drivers filled their tanks with fuel. A great migration of humanity began along the streets, and the sound of traffic filled the air.

A new day. And new opportunities for everyone. Ajit Hooda

stirred his tea and read in the newspaper about the gunshots fired in Dwarka the previous night. Ricky Talsera looked across the pillow at Shaalu, who was still asleep, overwhelmed by her tranquil beauty. Danny Khaneja stared down at the Indian Ocean from 35,000 feet and thought of his wife and son. Jaitendra held hands with Neha as they watched the Gangetic Plain drift by below them, the throbbing music of the helicopter like a symphony surrounding them. Hari Bhaiyya made his rounds of Building 3, checking the doors, looking at the log books. Shivani watched Jan DeVries walk across the rough-paved road to the departure area at IGI and wondered whether she would ever see him again. Down in Gurgaon, in a thousand different PG apartments, boys like Ravi and girls like Adita awoke to eat their humble breakfast, and then found their way to work. This great country, this young generation, headed uncontrollably towards the future. Every day there was only promise. There would be no looking back.

ACKNOWLEDGEMENTS

A work of fiction, modelled on the imagined happenings at a real place is unto itself a challenge. The task is even more daunting for an outsider, raised in the USA, who steps into an unfamiliar context like today's India and tries to give his tale a semblance of realism. The author is extremely grateful to the anonymous Delhi-based software executive who initiated this project and then provided all manner of support to aid in its completion. He, like the fictional Danny Khaneja, knew all the right people to call at the right time, and-fortunately for me-all the right doors effortlessly opened too. I owe a great debt of gratitude to the good people at an unnamed technology company in Gurgaon, who spoke candidly to me about their company, their work and their lives. They are justifiably proud of the business they have built and the fine work that they do; for the record, all names have been changed to protect the innocent: there was no Vikram doing dirty work by that or under any other name. All the crimes committed in this story are my own invention, wild speculations from an overactive imagination. Dr Manas Fuloria looked over the manuscript on its completion and added a wealth of constructive edits and comments, for which I am infinitely appreciative. A multitude of blessings on Rajat Verma, my prime consultant on all things about Delhi and Goa, the Indian underworld, the *challan* book, and how to obtain an exit visa; his friendship, experience, patience and connections filled in many gaps in my incomplete knowledge, lending an authenticity which a *firangi* could never hope to deliver. Mohan Narayanswamy of Travelscope India, sent me on a number of trips to the far reaches of Rajasthan, with incredible efficiency and style. The people at Aman Resorts also provided invaluable access to the rich culture found in remote areas, miles from the chaos of Delhi, and an especially memorable voyage to view the tigers of Ranthambhore. A special thanks to Simon Paterson, whose London pad became my halfway house on every trip east. Pooja Rajpal and the devoted staff at Shanti Home in West Delhi always provided a welcome place for the weary traveller to lay his head. The kids at Proton Business Schools of Indore and Ahmedabad helped me understand the dynamic young people who become the freshers that companies like Talsera hire, proponents of the India of tomorrow. Swami Gopal Buri and Swami Krishnanand of Rishikesh provided me with the gift of an unforgettable 60th birthday on the banks of the Ganga, in the low Himalayas. I am extremely grateful to the anonymous thief who stole my bag on the Derhadun train in July 2008, thus enabling me to see firsthand how an Indian police report was written, and then experience the Byzantine bureaucratic intricacies of the Foreign Residents Registration Office. John Schick of Portland, Oregon, was a faithful reader,

PrakashBook

offering encouragement and suggestions at every stage of the project. Daniel Weston helped me to understand the beauty and mysticism of code-writing and served as my prime software consultant. Paulina Borsook kept my digital awareness at a high technical level with her extraordinary expertise. Appreciation also goes out to Hans Ferdinand Degraeuwe of Bruges, Belgium, for his detailed dissertation on how the Nigerian scams work. I owe so much to the dedicated team at Fingerprint, who laboured over every excruciating detail contained here. Any cultural misfires are my own error and I apologise for any unintended offences, which are solely my own oversights and responsibilities. A world of thanks to Helen and Abe Michlin of Seal Beach, California, my loving parents, who patiently waited while their globe-trotting son made seven trips to India to do research for this novel, thousands of miles from home. And finally, a celestial wave to Donald D Moss (1913-1969), who would have been mightily pleased to see this humble novel in your hands today, dear reader.